A Rex Graves Mystery

MURDER
~ at ~
MIDNIGHT

C. S. Challinor

Large Print Edition
Other editions printed by Midnight Ink Books.

Cover art © AGCuesta at Can Stock Photo, Inc., 2017

Book cover design and formatting by Perfect Pages Literary Management, Inc.

ISBN-13: 978-1977938190
ISBN-10: 1977938191

REX GRAVES MYSTERY TITLES
IN LARGE PRINT

Christmas Is Murder
Murder at Midnight
Prelude to Murder
Say Goodbye to Archie
Say Murder with Flowers

Author's note: Liberty has been taken with the "disowned" Frasers, who were made up for fictional purposes and not meant in any way to impugn the illustrious Clan Fraser.

NB. The poem I made up, but to this day Jacobite gold is believed to be buried at Loch Arkaig, a location not far from Rex's retreat in the Scottish Highlands.

CAST OF MAIN CHARACTERS

Rex Graves—Scots barrister (advocate in Scotland) and amateur sleuth
Helen d'Arcy—his devoted fiancée from Derby, England
Julie Brownley—Helen's very single friend, a school teacher
Drew Harper—bachelor and house agent with seduction to spare
Alistair Frazer—Rex's legal colleague
John Dunbar—Alistair's partner, a paramedic
Flora Allerdice—a family friend from a previous case
Jason Short—Flora's boyfriend
Catriona Fraser—gullible heiress to Gleneagle Castle
Kenneth Fraser—Catriona's windbag husband
Dr. Humphrey L. Cleverly—professor of history at the University of Edinburgh
Margarita Delacruz—the professor's mysterious guest

Vanessa Weaver—snobbish interior designer

Ace Weaver—her disabled husband

Zoe Weaver—their actress daughter

Chief Inspector Dalgerry—Police Scotland detective at Lochaber, Skye and Lochalsh Area Command

~*~

Rex Graves QC & fiancée Helen d'Arcy
cordially invite you to join them in
celebrating Hogmanay
at Gleneagle Lodge, Gleneagle Village,
Inverness-shire in Scotland at eight pm
on the 31st of December.
RSVP

~*~

1
PORT IN A STORM

"The Allerdices are refurbishing the Loch Lochy Hotel," Vanessa Weaver informed Rex.

"Aboot time," he replied in his Lowland Scots burr, recalling with distaste the mouldy inn and fake hunting theme decor. "Has business picked up for them, then?"

"It has. Ever since the notoriety over the Moor Murders. Ghoulish, I know, that tourists would want to stay under the same roof as a serial killer... But there you are. I told Shona and Hamish the place needed a makeover, and I'm pleased to say they listened." Vanessa's green eyes gloated beneath her cloud of auburn hair.

"Well, no one can deny your talent and taste," Rex said graciously, taking in the expensive cut of the interior designer's purple velvet dress.

From across the living room came the sudden crash of breaking glass. Within the brief lull in conversation that followed, the stereo speakers could be heard playing a plaintive Gaelic ballad over the gale blowing fiercely outside the lodge.

"That Fraser woman dropped a glass," Vanessa muttered, referring to a dumpy, middle-aged redhead whose hair was a more muted shade than her own, though Vanessa's could not have been a natural colour at her age. "Now isn't breaking a glass bad luck?" The interior designer didn't wait for an answer. "It's because you and Helen have thirteen guests, just mark my words."

"I think that only applies to dinner parties," Rex said, keeping an eye on proceedings across the room. "In that case, we'd be fifteen, including Helen and myself. And if you're really worried, you could count Helen as a guest, which would make fourteen guests in total."

Vanessa humphed and took a sip of wine. Rex was about to assist his clumsy guest when his fiancée, a shapely blonde in a form-fitting black dress, waved him back, indicating she would deal with the broken glass herself.

Vanessa shook her head in disapproval. "That's why I never have parties in my home. Some people can't hold their drink—literally. I hope nothing spilt on that oriental rug I acquired for you. Especially blood."

Catriona Fraser had jumped up from removing shards of glass from the carpet and was holding her left thumb to her mouth. Alistair's partner offered his white cotton handkerchief. Helen, who had returned with a dustpan and brush, left again when she saw Catriona had cut herself. Rex in turn excused himself from Vanessa in order to fetch Mrs. Fraser a fresh drink.

"You were drinking whisky, correct?"

"I was, but fortunately the glass was empty, so none got on your lovely carpet. I'm so sorry about the glass. It was such a pretty tumbler with those etched thistles around the rim. Can I replace it?"

"No need. I have loads," Rex lied.

Helen returned with a cotton ball doused in disinfectant and a sticking plaster, and applied them to Catriona's thumb.

"So clumsy of me. I misjudged the table when I was putting the glass down, and it caught the edge and hit the floor."

Her husband put an arm around her thick waist. "Cat can hardly see out of her right eye, and has no depth perception," he explained.

"I tripped down the steps at the bar at the Glenspean Lodge hotel in

Roy Bridge one time. I hadn't even had a drink. It was horribly embarrassing."

"Happens to the best of us," Rex assured her, handing her a new glass filled with single malt and plenty of ice. She hadn't consumed more alcohol than anyone else, as far as he knew, but he decided to play it safe all the same.

His fiancée in her efficient way swept up the debris.

"Thank you, Helen," Catriona said, holding up her thumb wrapped in sticking plaster. "Sorry to be such a nuisance."

"Oh, nonsense," Helen replied with a warm smile. "It's nothing!"

Nothing compared to what had happened at his last party, Rex thought. He took the dustpan from Helen's hands. "You've done more than enough, lass." He planted a kiss on her neck and went to dispose of the shards in the kitchen.

The wind whistled at the window, wailing a banshee lament, pelting sleet against the glass with a vengeance. As Rex recalled, the keening fairy women in Scottish Gaelic mythology were tasked with washing the blood from the garments of those about to die. He gave an involuntary shudder at his reflection and turned away from the storm.

Back in the living room Rex continued his rounds with a cut-glass decanter of Glenlivet in one hand and a bottle of white wine in the other. His fiancée offered the guests a box of chocolates that someone had brought as a gift.

"Your Hogmanay party is a resounding success," she announced, glancing around the room where a dozen animated guests and one old man in a wheelchair sat by the roaring fire while the gale gathered in force outside. "Let's hope it doesn't all end in murder like last time," she added glibly, waving her wine glass.

Rex smiled at her. "Not like you to be such a pessimist." All the same, he felt a quiver of apprehension. His summer housewarming to celebrate the acquisition of his new retreat in the Highlands had ended in tragedy. He could only hope his New Year's Eve party would serve to sweep out the ghosts of the past and usher in a brighter future.

Two special guests from the housewarming event were present: Alistair Frazer, his colleague at the High Court of Justiciary; and Flora Allerdice, the daughter of the owners of the Loch Lochy Hotel, in whom Rex had taken an avuncular interest. He knew Alistair would have the delicacy not to refer to the murder at Gleneagle Lodge, and Flora certainly wouldn't, since it continued to be a painful memory for her.

The girl's looks had much improved since he first knew her. When he bought the lodge, she had been secretly in love with Alistair, not realizing that his attentions had been merely courteous. Properly in love at present, now that her brother required less of her attention, she had come into her own.

"It's wonderful to see her so happy," Helen said, as so often giving voice to his thoughts. "And Jason seems like a nice, steady boy." She looked over to where the young couple occupied a window seat in a bay window watching the sleet through the rattling panes. In the dark, Loch Lown was invisible, though on a clear day it took up the whole view.

"Flora told me they met at art college."

"That they did," Rex said. "She deserves some happiness after what she's been through in her short life.

Fortunately, her parents don't know she's here or I'd have had to invite them as well."

"Hamish Allerdice can't keep his hands to himself. Just think what he would have tried on with Julie."

Helen's friend was dressed to kill in a short plaid skirt and black leather boots. A gym-toned bleached blonde in her mid-forties, her attention was directed at Drew Harper. She had met him on a previous visit to the Highlands with Helen, and Rex had been at great pains to convince him to come to the party at both women's insistence. A man like Drew had no doubt been assailed by invitations from several females eager to snag that special New Year's Eve kiss, but Rex had prevailed.

The jade marble clock on the mantelpiece had just struck nine and the party was in full swing. Over the braying of the wind and the notes of a haunting melody arose the burble of conversation interjected by peals of laughter. The buffet prepared by Helen and Julie had been picked clean, and Scotch whisky flowed freely. The guests had brought shortbread and fruit cake, as well as streamers and noisemakers. These horns, whistles, and metallic fringed blowouts lay ready for midnight on the buffet table, lit by a ring-shaped iron candelabra holding twenty-four electric candles. Rex anticipated a loud and messy culmination to the festivities. However, it was Hogmanay, after all, and he hoped to make it a night to remember.

The living room, decked with scented candles and sprigs of holly and mistletoe, exuded an aroma of vanilla and pinewood smoke. Many guests had complimented him on the old-fashioned décor, and he had given Julie and Helen due credit for their part, once again. Mellowed by whisky, he began to truly enjoy himself and feel all would end well, after all.

Margarita Delacruz, a chic woman of indeterminate age, ebony hair pulled back in a chignon, placed her black sequined handbag among the pile by the party favours. She presented an exotic figure, her willowy form dressed from head to toe in black, a cashmere shawl thrown artfully over one shoulder, strands of amber beads and matching earrings adorning her person.

"I tried to engage her in conversation," Helen remarked. "From the little response I got, I think I detected the trace of a foreign accent."

"She's from South America, I believe. Perhaps she doesn't speak very good English. I'll take a crack at her later."

"Good luck. She and Professor Cleverly make a rather odd pair, don't you think?"

They had arrived together in his car. Humphrey Cleverly was now engaged in conversation with the debonair Alistair, a contrast in fashion and looks, the professor's gaunt frame clothed in a crumpled jacket, jeans, and an untidily knotted cravat, his head bald but for a closely shaved perimeter around the skull. And yet Rex knew better than to be fooled by his frumpy attire and awkward ways. The professor's intellect was as sharp as a razor blade.

"He and Margarita are just old friends, I gather. Humphrey dedicates most of his time to his dusty old books. He may have met her on his travels abroad." Cleverly's passion was socio-cultural anthropology, although he taught history at the University of Edinburgh. Rex continued his rounds, catching snatches of conversation.

"Six people called to say they felt unequal to braving the gale," Alistair was telling the professor in a less pronounced Scottish accent than the other men at the party, having been schooled at Eton. "I'm surprised so many actually managed to get here."

One couple had reported to Rex on the phone that they had made it as far as his entrance. The road then descended treacherously into the valley, where the lodge nestled by the almost frozen loch. They had decided to turn back before their car skidded on ice.

Hogmanay festivities in Scotland went on well into the wee hours, and he decided he would worry about what to do with his guests then, if the storm did not abate. He had enough rooms and plenty of food. Nor was there a shortage of firewood from the giant Scots pine uprooted in a previous gale, which he had chopped up and stored in the woodshed.

Julie, he saw, had managed to corner Drew. Absorbed in one another, they did not notice at first when Rex offered to refill their glasses. Perhaps Helen's match-making scheme would pay off after all, and Julie would conquer the seductive and soulful bachelor, who was the quintessential tall, dark, and handsome hero of romantic novels. Certainly, they had been inseparable the week of Julie's previous visit.

Less than three hours to go until midnight, he reflected, and presumably anybody who was going to come was already here.

"Thirteen guests, if this is all that's coming. Very unlucky," Vanessa Weaver repeated in her gentrified Scots while Rex replenished her wine glass.

The Scots were a superstitious lot. Part of "redding" the house for the New Year entailed whisking a broom around the rooms, burning cleansing juniper in the fireplace, and strewing mistletoe, hazel, and yew throughout to ward off evil spirits.

"Not much I can do aboot the unlucky number, Vanessa," he apologized, giving up on reasoning with her. Perhaps if she hadn't brought her daughter, whom he didn't remember inviting. Then there would have been twelve guests, excluding Helen. Vanessa had gushed earlier that night that Zoe was an actress and had recently auditioned for the part of a star-crossed lover in a television soap opera.

Zoe certainly looked tragic enough, brooding by the stone fireplace, obviously less than thrilled to be at the party, if not downright bored. Truth be told, there were no eligible men present, except for Drew Harper, and Julie had her claws well and truly into him, judging by the flirting going on between the pair at the far corner of the room. Still, if Rex were not mistaken, the house agent was not blind to Zoe's charms, and from time to time cast surreptitious looks in her direction. In her twenties, she possessed an arresting face and a tangle of reddish gold curls trailing down her bare-backed gown of emerald chiffon.

"Some guests were simply unable to make it in this weather," Rex explained to her mother. He wished Vanessa had been one of them. He had invited her because she had designed the interior of his lodge, and he had run into her in the village off-license. It had been obvious from the crates of liquor that he was preparing for a New Year's Eve party, and he had felt duty-bound to extend an invitation, thinking she would decline. She had an older invalid husband at home, a fact she had divulged when working on Gleneagle Lodge.

Miraculously, where others had failed, Ace Weaver had beaten the odds and, with the aid of a cane, had walked with excruciatingly slow steps down the frosty path to the door, where icicles dangled from the stone porch roof. Vanessa had brought his wheelchair from their station wagon and unfolded it by the fire, where he now dosed.

He had been an ace fighter pilot in the Second World War—hence the nickname—and perhaps it was this drive and spirit that had seen him through the inclement weather that showed no signs of abating.

2
THE UNWELCOME GUEST

"Ready for some more refreshment?" Rex asked the students tucked in the window seat. He recalled it was there Flora had sat with her brother, Donnie, on that previous occasion. He lifted the wine bottle and decanter in his hands to indicate the options.

"We're fine," Flora answered for them both. Her previously lacklustre dun hair shone in the soft lamplight, the bangs lifted back from her forehead in a barrette exposing her best feature, the misty grey eyes that now gazed adoringly on Jason. Her rosy cheeks dimpled as she said, "We still have two and a half hours to go until midnight, and we need to pace ourselves."

"Most sensible," Rex approved, thinking that some of his other guests could take a leaf out of the young couple's book. "We have soft drinks in the refrigerator. Just help yourselves."

"So kind of you to invite us. And thanks also for the wedding invitation." Flora suddenly looked worried. "Have you drawn up a list of preferred gifts yet?"

"Och, don't bother with that. I know how difficult it is for students financially. And at our age we have more toasters and fruit bowls than we know what to do with. Save your pennies—please!"

"Still, we'd like to get you something," insisted Jason, a sandy-haired and freckled lad.

"Well, how aboot one of your pictures, Flora, to hang at the lodge? We'd really appreciate that."

She brightened at once. "Jason can frame it! He's very handy."

"That's settled, then. Well, I'd better go and see to the fire. Scots pine burns quickly and it's almost out. Not too cold, are you?"

Flora, wrapped in a deep blue knitted shawl, shook her head no. The lad wore a thick sweater and, with the build of a rugby player, did not appear susceptible to the cold, even though Rex could feel a draught sneaking through the window. Behind the frosted panes, the wind continued its wailing and moaning lament.

"Oh, and keep the wedding invitation under your hats. We want to make it a small affair, and you know how these things can snowball."

Rex went to place a pine branch on top of the smouldering embers, the resinous needles, dead and dry, flaring abruptly. The old man stirred in his wheelchair, nodding off again before Rex could offer to fetch him something to drink, or apologize for waking him up with his fire-building activities. The pine smelled sharp and fresh. He watched the flames blaze for a moment before becoming aware of a presence behind him.

Margarita Delacruz, ramrod straight in her black calf-length dress and high heels, stood critically examining the painting of a red stag hanging above the mantelpiece as she lit her cigarette with a match from the box lying there.

Rex refrained from asking if she liked the picture, which was a fine copy of *Monarch of the Glen*, an oil-on-canvas by Sir Edwin Landseer, a protégé of Queen Victoria. It had replaced a real deer head staring mournfully down from the wall, a best-forgotten reminder that his house had once been a hunting lodge. He preferred to think of his valley retreat as a sanctuary, and enjoyed taking long walks through the pinewood forests and studying nature through a pair of binoculars rather than through the lens of a hunting rifle.

"Humphrey and I go far back," he

offered conversationally. "As I'm sure you know."

With a graceful turn of the neck, Margarita Delacruz redirected her attention to him. She was pale-skinned, unnaturally so, with contrasting dark eyebrows and scarlet lips painted in the shape of a bow.

"We were students together at Edinburgh," Rex pushed on. "I was studying law and Humphrey was a few years ahead of me, but we were on the same debate team."

"Yes," she said with a small smile, and took a long draw on her cigarette. It would have to be a long draw, Rex reflected, since the nicotine had to be inhaled all the way through the narrow holder. Furrows appeared above her mouth as she did so.

She exhaled with a delicate lift of her chin, the motion performed as though with long practiced art. Sweetly tanged tobacco smoke curled through the air. Rex, unusual for him, was at a loss as to what to say next. He tried another gambit.

"Have you been back from South America long? Ehm, where exactly in—"

"Not long," she said, waving a wisp of smoke away from her pale face. She might as well have been dismissing his words with the same gesture.

He felt he could hardly object to her cigarette since the fireplace was emitting its fair share of smoke. And no one else seemed to mind, even when Ken Fraser filled his pipe and lit it. The mood was jovial and made all the more cosy by the contrasting frigid fury raging outside. Just then, the wind howled in the chimney, sending the flames flickering wildly.

"What a night!" he declared to his reticent guest. "Well, let me know if you need anything!" he said in retreat, with all the blustering good cheer of the perfect host.

He caught Helen's I-told-you-so look from across the room and winked back at her. "Can we say Greta Garbo?" he murmured in passing, leaving his fiancée to chat with Alistair's partner, a dark-haired, tidy-featured paramedic in his late twenties, with whom she was discussing drug overdoses. A student counsellor at her high school, this would be a topic of interest for her. He left them to it.

"Who does the castle belong to now?" Alistair was asking the Frasers as they stood in a small group by a bay window pairing the one in which the students sat.

Rex's colleague cut a dashing figure with his chiselled nose and broad brow, his shaggy hair brushing the collar of an expensive wool suit. Rex had donned corduroys and a comfortable tweed jacket elbowed with leather patches, his attire *de rigueur* at the lodge. Even in their court wigs and black robes, Alistair managed to project an image of nobility, whereas Rex looked merely judicial.

"Gleneagle Castle belongs to us," Kenneth Fraser boasted.

"Really? I knew your name was Fraser but I thought it was a coincidence. So, you're the heirs apparent."

"The castle was in our family until a hundred years ago. Cat and I were able to reacquire it, along with the wee bit of land that abuts Rex's property."

"But what do you plan to do with it?" Alistair asked. "It's a ruin!"

Catriona hastened to agree. "But it was in the family for generations before it was lost in a gambling debt. Red Dougal built it in fifteen hundred and forty-six. We felt we had to get it back and uphold the family honour."

"Red Dougal?" Alistair enquired.

Catriona's husband took up the history of their ancestor. "Red Dougal of Clan Fraser. One part of the clan, under Red Dougal, refused to fight against the Camerons and the MacDonalds of Clanranald at the Battle of the Shirts, leaving their kin outnumbered two to one. The battle took place here in the Great Glen, at the head of Loch Lochy. The few Fraser survivors disowned their cowardly kin and chased Red Dougal and his defecting band from Inverness-shire. But they returned and took refuge in these glens, where they hunted and fished, and, according to family lore, made enough money from plundering outlying villages to build the modest castle you see up on the hill."

"Dougal MacNoodle," Alistair murmured in Rex's ear, a move facilitated by the fact that at six-two he stood only a couple of inches shorter than his host. "What guff!"

Rex shrugged non-committedly. He generally took people's family history with a grain of salt. However, he was not thrilled by the prospect of immediate neighbours, although making the old castle habitable would surely be cost-prohibitive.

"Are you going to renovate it?" Vanessa Weaver asked the new owners, homing in on the conversation with covetous interest.

Catriona and Ken glanced at each other mischievously. "That depends," Ken said.

Rex wanted to ask what it depended on, but Vanessa beat him to the punch. "I'm an interior designer, you know. I've done historic homes and grand hotels... Let me give you my card."

While she fluttered off to fetch one from her handbag on the table, Rex plied the Frasers' glasses with the Speyside whisky, going slightly easier on Catriona's after the earlier incident.

She beamed at him beneath her

greying auburn hair. "What a lovely party," she said. "And it's so nice to get acquainted with our neighbours." She declined the chocolates Helen offered, by way of explanation patting the extra padding around her waist.

Rex, for his part, selected a dark chocolate square from the confection-scented box, hoping for nougat or a creamy soft-centre. He would start on his diet tomorrow, on the first day of the coming year.

For the owners of a castle, the Frasers were pleasantly unpretentious, he reflected. Catriona's husband, in no way distinguished in bearing or looks, was growing tubby like his wife. He wore a navy-blue fisherman's sweater over black dress pants and a grey-and-white chequered muffler around his neck.

"So how did the castle end up back in your possession?" Alistair asked, his prosecutorial brain probing for the knotty details. "Drew was telling me there was a complex law of inheritance involved."

"And so there is," Catriona said. "We're distant cousins, Ken and I, the only surviving heirs of Red Dougal. There's an aunt Maighread to my first cousin, who sadly died of leukaemia, but no one's heard of her in a quarter of a century. And the law of inheritance, as it stood before the castle was lost, stipulated that the successor had to be not only a clan member but married within the clan, to ensure the property stayed within the family."

Alistair nodded thoughtfully. "Sounds like *mortmain*, a legal term from the French meaning 'dead hand,' which limits the granting of land outside an entity, in this case your Clan Fraser. Such a law often places a financial burden on the devisee, who is legally bound to keep the property."

"Well, that's the whole point," Catriona exclaimed. "The castle had to stay within the clan and couldn't be sold. The successive owners were unable to maintain it, and it fell into disrepair."

"But," said Ken, "an unscrupulous or skilful solicitor—depending on how you look at it—was able to transfer the castle out of the Frasers' hands by some consideration that did not involve actual money, for the satisfaction of a gambling debt. The case got convoluted, to say the least, but a judge finally ruled in our favour and we were able to get the castle back. The usurping owners only wanted it so they could boast they had a castle. They never did anything with it, as you can see."

"'Dead hand' is an apt description for restricting the transfer of property," Alistair opined. "You can just feel the weight of the dead hand controlling the destiny of the castle from the grave."

"Like a curse." Catriona Fraser nodded solemnly. "Red Dougal's dead hand."

"Aye, most interesting," said Rex, who normally liked nothing better than discussing the ins and outs of anachronistic legal terminology, but the tone of the conversation was turning morbid for a New Year's Eve party. Dead hands rising from the grave were better suited to Halloween.

He racked his brains for a more cheerful topic.

Ken Fraser raised a finger and spoke before Rex could think of one. "Moreover, it was a thorny legal point whether the old inheritance law still applied once the property had been forfeited. But to make a long story short..."

"Thank goodness," Vanessa Weaver said under her breath,

apparently waiting for a pause in the conversation so she could present her business card.

"The law was upheld. Catriona and I were happy to wed and comply in every respect."

"The old law didn't take into account what a family of profligates the Frasers were," his wife remarked.

"They really were," Ken added with relish. "I could tell you some stories—"

"Perhaps later," Alistair cut in, to Rex's relief. Ken Fraser was a windbag of the first order, as he had already demonstrated during the course of the evening.

"You're a Fraser, aren't you?" Helen asked Alistair.

"Frazer with a 'z,'" he specified. "It's possible, even probable that way back when, before clan lineage was properly recorded, we belonged to the same clan. In the olden days, there was one member in every clan community who was the official genealogist and could recite for hours on end who was the son of whom, and so on down through the generations. It can't always have been a reliable source."

"A sort of bard," Helen ventured.

"Exactly," Alistair said. "And hangers-on and servants often assumed, or were attributed, the chief's clan name, to add to the confusion."

"There would have been epic tales of exploits and derring-do, especially around the time of the Jacobite Rebellions," Ken Fraser enthused, adding ruefully, "before Bonny Prince Charlie fled 'over the sea to Skye.'"

"I visited the island of Skye as a child," Helen said. "I never realized its historical significance at the time. Didn't Prince Charles return to France afterwards?"

"He returned briefly to Scotland first," Ken replied. "But when all hope of putting him on the British throne was lost, he took a ship back to France; though he did send a spy to Scotland in seventeen fifty-three to find out where all his gold had disappeared to. The French had sent a fortune in payroll for his army," he explained, speaking mainly for the benefit of Helen, who might not have been so familiar with Scottish history, being English. "Spain also wanted a Catholic monarch in Britain and likewise shipped a vast amount of gold over to these parts to fund the Forty-Five Rising against the protestant Elector of Hanover."

"But much of it went astray," Professor Cleverly interjected slyly, smoothing down his bald pate. He'd had hair in college, quite a bit of it, recalled Rex, who had retained his, though the passage of time had faded the red to a more ginger hue.

"The treasure was entrusted to various clan chiefs," Cleverly continued in a professorial manner, peering through a pair of horn-rimmed spectacles perched upon his beakish nose. "Some of it was buried close to here," he informed Helen. "At Loch Arkaig just north of Fort William, and never recovered." He winked at the Frasers and said no more.

Rex looked at the couple expectantly. "Care to share what you know?" he asked.

"Well, it's really quite exciting," Ken took up again. "And it's mainly thanks to Humphrey that we are in possession of a valuable clue."

"A clue to the whereabouts of the treasure?" Cleverly's guest, Margarita Delacruz, exclaimed, her dark figure appearing as out of nowhere. It was the longest string of words Rex had yet heard her speak, and she delivered them with barely an accent.

"Now it must be said," Ken Fraser continued, as though wrapped up in the sound of his own pedantic voice and oblivious to her question, "that most of the clansmen took the secret of its location to the grave even under dire torture. One of the chiefs had his tongue cut oot!"

"How could he divulge the secret if his tongue was cut out?" Helen asked sensibly.

"The money was to go to helping Charlie's supporters escape the English Duke of Cumberland, known as The Butcher, and to aid those who'd been wounded at Culloden and dispossessed of their property. The survivors of the battle, which took place near Inverness, incidentally, hid oot in caves in the Highlands, and the loyal clansmen got money to them at great risk to themselves. The rest of the French gold was buried by the south banks of Loch Arkaig."

Rex was still waiting for the clue, which Ken, by design or distraction, was not being forthcoming in supplying.

"So, what was the clue?" Julie asked for him. She and Drew had been listening in on the conversation. By now, even the two lovebirds in the window seat were eavesdropping, as was Zoe, though pretending not to as she sat on the arm of a chair, swinging her foot beneath the hem of her green chiffon dress. Alistair's young partner had gravitated toward the group with his tumbler of twelve-year-old malt and stood beside the black-clad figure of Margarita Delacruz, who struck a theatrical pose as she listened intently to Ken, her black lacquer cigarette holder extended in one slender, manicured hand. Only Ace Weaver remained by the hearth, asleep in his wheelchair.

"I'm getting to that," Ken snapped, clearly wishing to proceed at his own pace and hold the floor for as long as possible.

"Sorry I asked," Julie retorted.

"Not all the Jacobites were as honourable, however. A Fraser, one of ours, I regret to say, was spying on the diggers and absconded with thousands of French guineas and gold bars, about ninety pounds' worth in weight, which he hid in a couple of beer kegs."

"Which was very ingenious," Catriona said. "Our ancestors were known to like their booze, so this was the perfect decoy!"

Everyone laughed except her husband, who attempted a smile but seemed annoyed by the interruption. "Fortunately, the thief died of gout before he could spend most of it. In a deathbed confession to his priest, he revealed that he had reburied the treasure he'd stolen from the loch."

"But where?" Alistair's partner asked, eyes wide with curiosity.

"Ah, John, we did not ken that until the priest's writings turned up in an estate sale last year. The family had kept the old papers in an antique chest, not thinking there was anything remotely important in them. Most of the stuff was in Latin and Gaelic. But Humphrey here, erudite historian that he is, was able to acquire them, at least temporarily, and translate them. The name Fraser came up in the priest's diary along with a description of the deathbed confession, and there was a poem in the collection, as well. The diary entry referred to a riddle that the dying Jacobite recited before he gasped his final breath."

"Well?" asked Margarita throwing up her hands in a Latin gesture of impatience. "Tell us the clue!"

"Humphrey, would you do the honours?" Ken asked pompously. "After all, you translated the poem."

"How thrilling," Zoe all but squealed.

Cleverly cleared his throat. "I'm no poet," he warned. "I took a few liberties with the Gaelic to keep it in rhyming verse, but I didn't change anything of substance." He cleared his throat again and paused. The room stood quiet in a brief respite from the storm, except for the crackling of the fire and the ticking of the mantelpiece clock, where the hour hand pointed to ten. Everyone held their breath, waiting for the professor to begin. Rex too was swept up in the historic tale of guilt and greed. The whereabouts of the Loch Arkaig Treasure remained one of the great unsolved mysteries of Scotland. Was it possible the people in this room were on the brink of discovering what had become of part of it?

Cleverly stared hard at the rug, slowly nodding as though in recollection. After a final decisive nod, he began the first words, but was cut short when a warbling voice from the fireplace recalled attention to the man in the wheelchair. Rex had assumed the invalid was asleep as, apparently, had the others, because everyone jumped.

"Closer, please, so I can hear. My ears aren't what they used to be."

"Very well," Professor Cleverly replied in surprise. "I'll stand here in the centre, so everybody can hear." Accustomed to giving lectures, he began for the second time, addressing the entire room, where everyone listened spellbound.

3
A GAELIC POEM

Seek high, seek low
For the Jacobite gold
Brought over the seas in a stout
ship's hold
A princely sum raised by France
and Spain
That bonny brave Scotland might
fight again.
Hidden in the glen where the eagle
soars
Above the loch where the burn in
spring roars
For forty-odd years buried long and
deep
How many more years its secret to
keep?

A brief silence ensued, and then everyone began talking at once.

"I don't see any specific clues," Julie said, slightly the worse for drink and slurring her words.

"Don't you?" the professor asked with a sly smile amid his grey stubble.

"It's all in the words *glen, eagle, buried* and *keep*," Catriona explained. "As in the keep of a castle. Gleneagle Castle."

"It's pretty obvious when you know the location," Rex agreed. "'Above the loch where the burn in spring roars,'" he quoted. "When the ice melts in spring, that burn runs swift and positively clamours."

Helen alone seemed to appreciate the sarcasm in his words, and cast him a knowing look, suppressing a smile.

"Exactly," Catriona exclaimed in triumph. "It's clear as daylight. And we know the gold came to the west coast of Scotland, not far from here."

"But," said Flora. "Sorry to put a damper on things... Glens, lochs, eagles, and even castles, are common in Scotland. And castles were often built on hills and near streams."

"But the priest's diary refers to a Fraser from these parts," the professor countered. "'A laird plagued by the shame of his forebears,' an entry reads, 'who could not escape his dark and cowardly destiny of betrayal and deceit.'" Cleverly succeeded in instilling the most sinister sentiment into his quote. "A man who stole from the Young Pretender and his loyal and brave followers. It was fitting that he died before he could enjoy all his gold." He shook his bald head and gave a heartfelt sigh. "The curse of the Red Dougal Frasers."

"This is giving me goose bumps," Helen said, rubbing her bare arms.

The professor, brusquely swivelling his red paisley cravat out of the way, set down his tumbler of whisky on the nearest table and put himself in a semi-crouch, hands open before his face, as if warding off danger. "Imagine the clansman, swathed in tartan stained with sweat and soiled with the earth, digging up bags of gold from the loch-shore, where he'd previously marked the spot by carving out a cross with his dirk in the bark of an alder tree. Perhaps he wore a white cockade on his bonnet, the emblem of the Jacobites." Cleverly stopped his mime of digging and cupped a hand to his ear, as though listening out for the sound of voices echoing across the purple glen or horses trampling through the fallen leaves of the valley. The guests stared at him owlishly, captivated by his description of the furtive robber.

"He digs under cover of darkness, afraid of the sound his spade makes sluicing and scraping into the ground, afraid of the whistling of mallard wings over the loch. To be caught means certain death, a traitor's ignominious and terrible death. After hours of digging he hides the bags in his beer kegs, which he straps either side of a mule. Then, leaving the hiding place as though nothing ever was, he takes to the forests and hills, hiding from English soldiers and from his own kith and kin until, finally, he reaches his castle. He dares not rest until his clinking cache of glittering gold is safely buried once more, this time deep under the flagstones of the keep."

The professor took a curt bow to indicate his story was concluded, and received a hearty applause. Jason tooted loudly with a paper blowout he had brought to the party.

"Everyone's in high spirits," Rex commented to Helen with the satisfaction of a successful host.

"Spirits is right," she said pointedly, her glance sweeping the empty bottles on the table.

Cleverly resumed in his professorial tone, "The Highland clans-folk among whom Prince Charlie sought refuge never betrayed his whereabouts to the government troops, even though a fortune in bounty was offered on his pretty head."

He stroked his own pate, but whereas the Young Pretender had been famed for his fair curls, Cleverly could only feel scalp. "And no one knew what to do with all the gold once Charlie left, although many hoped he would return to attempt another armed action. Enough gold to sink a ship had been delivered to Loch nan Umah, seven or eight barrels of it aboard the *Bellona*, each containing five thousand gold pieces, the total worth over ten million pounds today, an astounding sum back then. Much of it simply vanished into thin air." He performed a conjuring motion with his hand. "Until now, that is."

"To excavate the gold, always assuming it's buried in the keep, as the poem suggests, would cost an arm and a leg," Alistair contended. "And there's no real guarantee that it's there."

"Perhaps Jason can assist you with that," Drew Harper said, levelling a look at the student.

"What do you mean?" Jason demanded.

"Why don't you tell all us curious people what you found there?" Drew's sombre blue eyes challenged him unflinchingly.

Jason's mouth formed an angry line as he glared back at the house agent. "Why don't you mind your own business?" he blurted after a brief pause.

"What's going on here?" Alistair stepped between the two men, both of them athletic; but whereas Jason was stocky, Drew was tall and lean. "Stop being so obscure, Drew. If you know something relevant to the subject of the alleged buried gold, cough it up, why don't you."

"I will, if Jason won't. I just wanted to give him the opportunity to come clean."

"Jason?" Flora began questioningly behind her boyfriend.

He held her back. "Come clean?" he returned, staring Drew down. "You make me sound like a criminal."

"I'm sorry, but stealing is a criminal activity."

Rex decided to intervene at this point. Tempers were rising, and he didn't want the mood at his party to sour. "I'm sure there is a perfectly reasonable explanation for this. Jason, lad, why don't you tell us in your own words what Drew is referring to and lay this possible misunderstanding to rest?"

"Hear, hear," said Ken, availing himself of more Scotch.

With a contemptuous glance at the house agent, Jason told how, being a metal detector enthusiast, he had walked over the glen from the Loch

Lochy Hotel, where he and Flora had been staying one weekend in the autumn to visit her family. It had been a breezy day, and Flora had wanted to spend time with her brother Donnie, whom Jason explained to those of Rex's guests who might be unaware, was learning-disabled and very close to his sister, with whom he shared a special bond. Flora nodded with a tender expression in her wistful grey eyes. Anyway, Jason went on, gaining confidence, he had decided to go on a hike and taken his metal detector with him, because you never knew what ancient artefacts and weapon parts you might find in this remote area. Professor Cleverly murmured assent. Jason had seen Rex's "No Trespassing" and "Hunting Strictly Prohibited" signs, but none had been in evidence up by the castle, and so he had switched on his metal detector and begun a search around the castle walls and inside the ruins.

"You found something?" Catriona interrupted, electrified.

Jason nodded gravely. "I did. In a sort of gutter leading out from the wall of the keep, deeply buried in mud and dead leaves. The detector gave off a signal and I started to dig. I had brought a trowel and a bag with me in case I found anything."

"And what was it?" Ken asked with a crack in his voice.

"Well, it was a golden guinea, a French *louis d'or!*" The Frasers both gasped. "I rubbed off the dirt and almost fainted when I saw the engravings. The head of Louis Fifteenth on one side, and a triple fleur-de-lys and the date seventeen hundred-and-forty on the other. When I got back to the burn, I rinsed it clean and it gleamed yellow in the sun. It was the most amazing thing ever, to hold something whole and precious in your hands that no human had touched for centuries," Jason whispered the sentence with reverence.

The Frasers hugged each other. Margarita Delacruz crossed herself while the professor nodded in perfect understanding of Jason's words. "Untouched rebel gold," he mused aloud.

"It must have escaped from one of the laird's bags," Catriona uttered. "Or maybe he dropped it..."

"That's why you were so excited when you got back to the hotel," Flora said to Jason, resentment cutting into her voice. "Why didn't you tell me?"

Her boyfriend shrugged in apology. "I don't know."

"I do," said Drew. "It's illegal to keep any ancient coins you find. You're supposed to turn them over to Treasure Trove in Scotland."

"It was just one coin."

"One historical gold coin," Drew

corrected.

"But where there's one coin, there may be others, eh?" Professor Cleverly addressed the Frasers.

"Did you search anywhere else?" Ken asked Jason eagerly.

"I stayed at it for another hour, but not a beep. I had to get back to the hotel in time for dinner, and Flora and I headed back to Inverness in the morning. I'll return the coin to you," he told the Frasers sheepishly. "I've never taken anything that didn't belong to me before."

"We didn't own the castle in the autumn," Catriona told him. "We only took possession three weeks ago. The coin doesn't really belong to us, or does it? Does he have to give the coin up, Rex? Alistair? You're the legal experts."

"But I'm not a policeman," Rex said. "I'll not report it. Let this young man's conscience be the judge."

Alistair held out his palms in front

of him. He didn't want to get involved either.

"What about the previous owners?" Drew asked.

"Why should you care?" Jason demanded. "Were you spying on me that day? Come to think of it, what were *you* doing there?"

"My job," Drew replied evenly. "Isn't it strictly the previous owners' property?" he went on, addressing the gathering, "and shouldn't they be the ones to return it to the Crown?"

"Or to France?" the professor suggested smugly. "It came from French coffers, after all."

"I think the boy should just keep his coin," Señora Delacruz surprised everyone by stating. "Much simpler, no?"

"How much is one of these French louis worth?" Julie enquired.

Professor Cleverly clutched his chin as he did a mental calculation. "A golden guinea was equal to thirteen pounds Scots in old money, so, let me see... Between two and three hundred pounds in actual value today? But historical value? Almost priceless if it is part of the Jacobite Gold." He opened his arms wide. "Reputedly, there were not only louis of France, but crusadoes of Spain and English guineas donated to the Jacobite cause, as well. The location of the gold was kept secret in the hope of another rising in Scotland, but with the passing of Charles Edward Stuart in seventeen hundred and eighty-eight, all hope was finally lost." Humphrey gazed at nothing in particular as though caught in the past.

"Here's to a new chance at Independence," John said brightly, clinking glasses with Alistair and Jason. "No offence to the Sassenachs here...," the medic added, referring to the two English ladies from Derby.

"None taken," Helen said

cheerfully. "We're very pro Scotland, aren't we, Julie?"

"Definitely," her friend replied, sneaking a glance at Drew's handsome profile. Helen and Julie exchanged knowing glances, Drew clearly oblivious to the forces at work on his future.

Glasses were refilled. The mood around the fire grew more animated still. Crystal clinked and toasts were made.

"The gold has to be there, don't you see?" Catriona said, unable to drop the subject. "Buried in the keep like the poem says. Now, thanks to Jason, we have proof!"

Jason smiled, while Drew scowled.

"How come your ancestors never found it?" Vanessa asked. She and her daughter had been quiet for much of the discussion, but had paid close attention. Ace Weaver had dosed off after Professor Cleverly recited the poem, and no one seemed to give him another thought.

"They tried," Catriona replied. "They all but tore the castle apart looking for it. But it must be buried really deep under the flagstones. Or else they didn't know where to look. The ground will have to be dug up."

Rex inwardly groaned at the thought of the heavy equipment that would be brought into the valley, no doubt at the expense of several trees. He had bought Gleneagle Lodge to get away from noise and disturbance and crowds of people. Now he would have to postpone his weekend and holiday visits until the work was completed. No doubt nature would flee as well. The news did not bode well for the coming year. He was almost sorry he had thrown a party. Bad news could wait, and certainly had no place ruining his Hogmanay celebrations.

"Don't worry, Rex," Helen consoled him in an undertone. "It may never happen."

"It could be a fool's errand," Alistair warned the Frasers. "One of your ancestors may have already found the gold and spent it."

"That cannot be the case," Ken argued, his mouth a small square in his short-clipped grey beard. "The family fortune would have been restored, and clearly it wasn't. Malcolm Fraser was a miser and would not have told anybody of its exact location. Many a clan member went mad or suicidal from despair looking for it."

"The inbreeding would have accounted for much of the insanity," Alistair remarked to general amusement. Even the Frasers took his comment in good spirit. Margarita Delacruz crossed herself again.

"The treasure came to be a curse, to be sure," Ken Fraser related. "But for the gold, the clan would have gone about their business and continued to thrive instead of staking all on a gamble. The priest mentions gold bars or ingots in his journal. These possibly came from Spain."

"Gold bars don't fall under the same category as coins, do they?" Jason asked.

"Finders keepers in this case, I believe," Alistair opined, consulting Rex with a look of inquiry.

"Might depend on what markings, if any, they have on them."

"What I couldn't do with a fortune in gold," Jason exclaimed dreamily.

"Keep your envy in check, lad," Ken returned. "A Gaelic proverb tells us it is the second cousin of avarice and wears the same tartan. Besides," he added with moist eyes, "your youth is your wealth. I envy you that, I'll not deny it."

Booze made some men maudlin, Rex reflected. By the time Auld Lang Syne rolled around, there would be tears indeed.

Catriona linked her husband's arm. "Cheer up, Ken, sweetie. This promises to be the best year yet for the both of us."

Rex raised his glass. "You certainly have plenty to look forward to. Best of luck!"

Everyone voiced their agreement. The cousins were married as required by Fraser law to inherit the castle and all it contained, even if the prospect of children seemed remote at their age. What would happen to the castle then, with no one left in the dissenting clan of old? Still, Ken and Catriona seemed happy enough for a marriage of convenience, Rex reasoned, and he genuinely wished them the best.

"And to Rex and Helen, and their forthcoming nuptials!" Alistair toasted in turn.

"And maybe something in the offing for this young pair." Rex raised his glass to the students. "Jason and Flora!"

"Jason and Flora!" everyone chorused.

The students smiled shyly at each other. Rex, taking this opportunity to go to the bathroom, headed upstairs. The cloakroom at the far end of the hall downstairs had been prepared for the guests' use.

Well, well, he reflected. All this talk about hidden treasure and it transpiring that Jason had a piece of it! Strange that the lad hadn't told Flora. Perhaps he had thought her father would find out, and Rex couldn't blame him for not trusting the boorish Hamish. And what was Drew Harper's beef with Jason?

Rex found the house agent's holier-than-thou attitude somewhat bemusing. He had sounded like a chiding school master! *Well, best get back to the fray*, he thought cheerfully, soaping his hands in the basin. The tension had died down between Jason and Drew, but he preferred to be in the living room keeping the peace in case tempers erupted again.

"What if someone finds out about the gold and steals it?" Vanessa was asking the Frasers when he returned to the living room carrying a platter of smoked salmon canapés edged with watercress. It would soon be time to serve the champagne. "I mean, it's a huge temptation," she pursued darkly.

Rex wondered if the subject of the missing treasure would ever be dropped that night, but everyone had tuned in to the conversation with renewed interest.

"We've posted armed gillies aboot the place," Ken Fraser said. "And put up no-trespassing signs. That should keep any fortune hunters at bay. But hardly anyone kens aboot the gold."

"They do now," Señora Delacruz

pointed out, indicating the room at large. "And if it's as much gold as you say, I'm not sure a pair of gamekeepers and their shotguns will act as much of a deterrent."

"How did you know th-" But Ken was cut off mid question by a loud and distressed gasp.

Everyone looked over to where Drew Harper was clutching his throat, alternately struggling to loosen his tie and trying to cough or retch. He had grown alarmingly red in the face and his eyes bulged. Rex's first thought was poison. Julie started shrieking and gesticulating wildly.

"I knew something like this would happen," Vanessa Weaver cried out in vindicated glee.

Alistair's partner, John, was beside Drew in an instant, acting upon professional reflex while the others stood by in shock, except Rex who had moved in almost as quickly.

"Is he choking on something?" John asked Julie.

She pointed to the box of chocolates on the table. John immediately got behind the house agent and, grabbing him around the waist, performed the Heimlich manoeuvre, whereupon a small projectile issued from Drew's mouth.

John picked it up from the floor. "It's a hazelnut," he said examining it.

Drew, visibly relieved, almost laughing now, said, "It went down the wrong way."

Julie said she would fetch him some water and rushed to the drinks cabinet.

"Close call, mate," Jason said, with just a hint of satisfaction on his face. He probably thought Harper had received his just desserts for calling him out on misappropriating the gold coin.

"All's well that ends well," Ken

exclaimed, beaming at everyone, filled tumbler in hand. His face was ruddy and he had untied his chequered scarf so the ends fell either side of his navy sweater.

Of the men, he seemed the most affected by drink. Jason, the jock, was holding his own, and John Dunbar had been mostly abstemious, having declared himself the designated driver when it came time for him and Alistair to leave. Drew Harper had been coddling his third whisky for a while now. The women, all on wine, except for Catriona, were merry. Rex was keeping an eye on Julie, though he knew Helen would be too. Her friend had had a serious breakup earlier in the year and was feeling, as Helen put it, "fragile." Hence the two getaways to Gleneagle Lodge and the combined assault on Drew Harper. Rex gave a sigh. Perhaps it was too soon for Julie. She was on the rebound and clearly smitten by the attractive bachelor. Hopefully her infatuation would not be unrequited.

"Lucky we had a medic in the house," Alistair said proudly, clapping John on the shoulder.

Lucky it wasn't anything more serious, Rex thought, recalling the murder at his housewarming party.

4
RESOLUTIONS

"Time for a party game," Julie announced giddily.

She had laddered her black tights above her boot and appeared a bit flushed, either from excitement or else too much drink. Rex again wondered about the wisdom of letting Helen set her up with Drew, who was beginning to cast around for a means of escape.

Rex caught Helen's eye and communicated his concern with a slight nod in Julie's direction coupled with a worried look. Helen crossed the room to join him. "Julie is just letting her hair down. She won't make a fool of herself in front of Drew."

"I hope not," he said.

"Here's my idea," Julie followed up when she had everyone's attention. "We all write down our New Year resolutions and entrust them to Rex.

Then, at the end of the year, we can see how we did!"

"Are these resolutions to remain private?" John asked.

"They could be... But wouldn't we be more likely to keep our resolutions if everyone knew about them? And it would be more fun. A bit like a game of Truth or Dare? We can sit around the table by the fire where there's more light."

"I suppose we could just lie." John obviously opposed the idea.

"That's hardly entering into the spirit of things," Vanessa Weaver retorted with a laugh. "I'm game." She looked about her. "Has anyone got a pencil and paper?"

Cleverly produced a couple of writing implements from the recesses of his creased jacket, one a sharp pencil, the other an elegant capped pen, which he set down in the middle of the oblong coffee table that was carved in oak. Jason came up with a disposable ballpoint pen with no nib. "Well, this Biro is useless," he said, frowning and returning the empty plastic tube to his pocket. "Wonder why I kept it."

"Because you never throw anything away," Flora reminded him fondly, the incident regarding the gold coin apparently forgotten.

"I'll get what we need." Rex strode down the hall to his library and gathered a fistful of pens and pencils, and a pair of scissors. He grabbed a couple of sheets of thick cream notepaper headed with *Gleneagle Lodge* in elegant black script, along with the address and land-line number. He then returned to the living room and added his assortment of writing tools to the collection, folded the two sheets of notepaper, and cut them into small rectangles. He directed everyone to write their name on the back. The rest of the guests approached the table and brought extra chairs as necessary, chatting with excitement.

"I don't remember ever making my New Year resolutions public," Flora fretted.

"Why worry?" asked Jason. "Unless it's really embarrassing." He nudged his girlfriend in the ribs.

"Mine's not, particularly," Zoe said. "I just wonder if they'll come true if we speak them aloud."

"They're resolutions, not wishes," Margarita Delacruz said with a shrug, and took an elegant puff of her elongated cigarette.

"And what do the resolutions of our gracious hosts entail?" asked Cleverly. "They should have the honour of going first." When nobody contested this, he said, "Rex?"

Spending more time at this place, Rex thought. *Without any blasted interruptions*. He wrote the first part down and communicated it to the gathering around the table. He enjoyed coming to Gleneagle Lodge to relax and sometimes work on a difficult case, and to spend quiet time with Helen roaming the countryside or else skiing.

"Good one," said Jason.

"And Helen?" the professor prompted.

"A beautiful spring wedding," she said without hesitation and wrote on her piece of paper.

"I'm sure it will be," Flora assured her. "I'm so very much looking forward to it."

"We'll go in order," Julie dictated, nodding at John seated to Helen's right on the large sofa resting against the wall.

"Mine is to give up smoking," said the medic. "I mean, I've quit, but I plan to stay off cigs for good this time. Alistair can't abide smoking." John winked at him across the table.

"Plus, it doesn't reflect well when you're an ambulance man," the Scottish advocate teased his partner. "Treating people for strokes and nicotine poisoning. You need to set an example."

Alistair and John had met at Rex's weekend housewarming party. It was John's ambulance that had removed the body. Rex tried to console himself that at least a new romance had blossomed out of the tragedy.

Señora Delacruz tapped her ash into a heavy glass bowl and said, "I only smoke socially." Which was rather *anti*social in Rex's, the reformed pipe smoker's, opinion. Her slim black cigarette holder created an arc of smoke.

Rex got up and opened a side window just a crack as he went to change the compact discs in the stereo system. He selected a compilation of Scottish dance music with an upbeat tempo to keep his guests awake for the last hour or so until midnight.

"Quitting is hard," Ken Fraser commiserated with John. "I've managed to cut down on my pipe, but I've put on weight as a result."

"I'm with you there," Rex said, crossing to the bay windows. He kept his pipe in his pocket out of habit, and found comfort in fingering it in times of stress. On a few dire occasions, he had come to within a hair's breadth of lighting up and taking a heavenly puff.

He glanced out the dark window. Sleet was driving into the canted panes, pinging relentlessly on the glass. He imagined a trespasser peering through the lit windows at the revellers within, and it gave him an uneasy sense of foreboding. He hastily drew the burgundy velvet drapes and returned to the group seated around the coffee table.

"Well, on the subject of weight,

that's my resolution." Catriona vowed to join a gym and lose half a stone. She made a note on her paper and handed her pencil to Ken seated in an adjoining armchair.

"Easy. My resolution in the coming year is to find the gold," her husband proclaimed as he wrote. "Almost one and a half million pounds!" He let the pencil drop on the table and rubbed his hands with glee.

Everyone, clearly envious, wished him good luck, even if he couldn't keep the coins. But perhaps there were gold bars among the treasure, as Professor Cleverly had indicated, citing the priest's diary.

"As for me, I hope to make head of department," Cleverly said, whose turn it was to state his resolution. "Lord knows, I've waited long enough."

"True," Rex agreed. The professor had taught at the University of Edinburgh since obtaining his doctorate, without any substantial advancement. It was his time, and Rex wished his old college friend well.

"You deserve it, Humpty," Señora Delacruz stated from across the table. Humpty? thought Rex with mirth. "You have published more than Peebles and what's that other pompous ass's name?" She waved her hand airily. "They will be forgotten. But your research will live on."

"Thank you, my dear," Professor Cleverly acknowledged with a bow of the head.

"Zoe, it's your turn," Helen reminded the young woman, who showed reluctance to speak.

"I'm really afraid if I say it aloud, I'll jinx it." Zoe smiled most becomingly in her shyness. Her face, though a trifle long, held undeniable charm. Curled up in the capacious armchair in her filmy green dress, she was the picture of youth and loveliness. The effect was not lost on the house agent. Rex caught Drew staring at her with admiration just a moment too long. Julie noticed too and pinched her lips.

"Poppycock," said the professor. "You are a modern young woman, are you not, Zoe? Leave the superstitious voodoo to the old and ignorant."

Zoe twiddled a long tendril of reddish-gold hair that flamed in the firelight, her secret playing on curvaceous lips.

"We've told ours," John egged her on, holding up his piece of paper. "Written for posterity to take note of."

"Go on, Zoe," Jason seconded. "Everybody else has been spilling their guts."

"It can't be as lame as mine," Flora encouraged her.

"Well, okay, then." Succumbing to the pressure of her peers, Zoe said in a rush, "My resolution, or dearest wish, is to get the part of Wild Rose that I auditioned for before Christmas." She blushed and darted a hopeful look at her mother.

"Ooh, how exciting," Flora exclaimed. "No one told me you were an actress. Is it a play or a film?"

"It's for a miniseries airing on ITV. Wild Rose is the female lead part and also the title. It's about two feuding families in the Highlands. Wild Rose is in love with Jack MacBride, the neighbouring landowner's son, but their parents are bitterly opposed to their relationship, and they have to meet in secret on the moor."

"Sounds like a cross between *Romeo and Juliet* and *Wuthering Heights*," Alistair remarked pleasantly.

"It is a bit soapy, I suppose," Zoe trailed off with obvious misgivings about divulging her New Year's resolution.

"Oh, not at all," Helen hastened to assure her. "It sounds just the sort of thing Julie and I like to watch with a glass of wine after a gruelling day at the school. I love romance. And set in the Highlands! How perfect."

Helen's friend did not look as enthusiastic, Rex noted; probably because Drew was watching and listening with avid interest.

"I teach geography, and Helen is a school guidance counsellor," Julie explained to Zoe in an obvious attempt to regain his attention.

"Any notable actors going to be in it?" the house agent asked Zoe.

"There's a rumour going about, and it is only a rumour, mind, that a famous actor will play the detective. Rose and Jack discover a body, but they can't say anything because they weren't supposed to be out together, especially at night. There's a series of mutilated bodies, actually—all young females."

A serial killer on the moor, Rex

thought, unpleasantly reminded of events he would have preferred left out of the conversation.

"Jack the Ripper," Alistair suggested, seemingly adamant on drawing parallels. Rex glared at his colleague in an attempt to silence him. Had he forgotten the nightmare they had both been involved in that summer?

"I hope you get the part," Jason said. "Then we can all say we knew you before you were a celebrity."

"I think she will," said her mother. "She has the face, body, and talent."

"I have to play an eighteen-year-old, though," Zoe informed her audience. "And I'm twenty-four, almost."

"You could pass for eighteen," Drew said appraisingly.

Julie shot him a stricken look, her cheeks colouring slightly. A woman well into her forties, she would feel threatened by a willowy young beauty when a seductive man like Drew was at stake. Rex knew for a fact he jogged four miles each day. And the touch of silver at his temples only served to lend distinction to his lean-featured good looks.

"Women can pass for much younger with a little *savoir-faire."* Margarita Delacruz winked with allure, and Rex could tell the women and some of the men were dying to ask her age. However, good manners prevailed, and the party game continued with Alistair.

"I'm such a dunce at party games!" he despaired, looking around for inspiration. He apparently thought he might find some in his tumbler of whisky, the rest of which he downed in one gulp. "Um-um-um. Yes, I'm going to catch the Loch Ness Monster. That's it!"

"Pathetic," John said, shaking his head at his partner. "For a start, you've got no chance. And you'd think with your brains you could come up with something better."

"It doesn't even exist," Margarita Delacruz scoffed. "It's nothing but a tourist gimmick."

"Someone saw a sea monster like Nessie in Loch Lochy," Flora informed her.

"Nonsense."

"We took a photo of it from the dining room window at the hotel."

"A trick of the light or a log maybe?"

"Well, if Alistair wants to go chasing figments of the imagination, that's his business," Rex said, eager to press on with the parlour game as the hands on the clock face moved inexorably towards midnight. "We can remind him of his folly twelve months hence. Flora, lass, please give us something sensible."

"I resolve to spend more time with

my brother, even though I'm really busy with my art courses and my part-time work at the coffee shop," she added apologetically.

"You said earlier your resolution was silly, Flora," Vanessa Weaver said. "But taking care of your brother is commendable." She cast a tender look at her husband's motionless body in his wheel chair, and Rex warmed towards her. The Scottish whisky, with its distinctively clean, almost medicinal taste, made him feel expansive, and he viewed his guests with good will, hoping all their resolutions came true.

"And I'm going to work hard on finishing my sculpture," Flora's boyfriend continued beside her. "I'm sculpting a room-size space shuttle."

"What is it made of?" enquired Helen, who had a genuine affinity for young people, one of many qualities Rex appreciated about her.

"All reclaimed materials," Jason

replied. "Egg cartons, coat hangers, duct tape, yoghurt lids, you name it."

"Jason can make stuff out of nothing," Flora said. "He's brilliant."

"My dad doesn't think so. He has a chemist shop and wanted me to follow in his footsteps, but all that pill-counting and selling cough drops and bath salts didn't appeal in the slightest."

"I expect he just wanted you to have a secure future," Alistair said in the father's defence. "I wanted to become an artist, but my father persuaded me otherwise. I think it was the right decision, in retrospect. But kudos to you for sticking to your guns."

Everyone next turned towards Señora Delacruz. What would the intriguing lady come up with?

"Ah, this is so difficult...," Margarita began. "Perhaps keep on doing what I have been doing so far? Travelling to remote parts, exploring cultures. But, yes, maybe something artistic, too. Perhaps I shall take up water colour in the coming year."

Rex couldn't speak for all the guests, but he could tell by the expressions on one or two faces that they felt mildly let down. Painting in water colour seemed a bit undramatic for a person of such striking presence and personality, whom he could readily picture dancing the tango.

"Well, I plan on winning Interior Designer of the Highlands this coming year," Vanessa Weaver burst out, clearly anxious for her turn. "It's a very prestigious award and brings in a lot of work."

"How do you go about achieving that?" Flora asked, reaching for her glass of ginger ale on the table.

"You submit a design board of your best project for the year. That would be my work on the Georgian mansion in

Ardnamurchan-And-Ardgour. If you make the cut, the judges visit the property. Then, if nominated, you're invited to a ball at Glenspean Lodge, where the winner is announced."

"Don't trip on the steps there if you're wearing a long dress," Catriona warned. "That's what I did."

"How about that actress tripping at the Oscars," Jason jeered.

"I would have been mortified," said Zoe. "But she collected herself with great dignity, I thought. It's what you have to do."

"I plan to get out of this chair more," Ace Weaver declared from his corner by the fire, much to everyone's amusement.

"Thought you were asleep, dear, or I'd have brought you to the table."

"Just resting with my eyes closed," he informed his wife.

"He does that," she told those circled around the table. "He takes everything in. You see he didn't miss his turn. Comes from being a fighter pilot in the war, I suppose. He's always on the alert."

This time no response came from the corner. Ace Weaver had checked out again.

"Is that everybody?" Rex asked. "Oh, Julie, you're up, aren't you? For some reason I thought you'd started."

"I intend to snag a husband in the coming year, pure and simple. Helen's getting married and I want to as well!" Julie practically wailed.

She looked as though she might burst into tears, but recovered in time. Everyone paused in stunned silence, and then began to offer advice and encouragement, all but Drew who almost imperceptibly moved away from her on the loveseat.

"You, now," she said twisting towards him with shiny blue eyes.

"I plan on beating the record in

home sales I set for myself at the beginning of this year. The market's been a bit depressed, but I did okay considering. Next year will be better." Drew raised his tumbler in a toast.

More banter and encouragement followed around the table, while Julie rolled her eyes at Helen. *Men!* The guests began to hand their slips of paper to Rex.

"What is it I'm supposed to do with these again?" he asked, gathering up the resolutions, ranging from love to greed.

"Oh, just stick them in a jam jar and put them somewhere safe," Julie suggested. "At the end of next year, you can remind each of us of our resolutions and find out if we succeeded or not."

"What about a prize for the person who came closest to their goals?" Jason said.

"Fair enough. Well, good luck

everybody, and thank you, Julie, for suggesting this fun enterprise."

Everyone clapped except for Ace Weaver. Rex made a neat pile of the pieces of paper, including the one Vanessa had written on her husband's behalf. The invalid's hands lay knotty and arthritic in his lap, which was draped over with a traveling blanket. His walking stick stood propped against the side of the fireplace within arm's reach, but it didn't look as though he planned on going anywhere for a while.

"Oh gracious, is that the time!" Helen nudged Rex.

The mantelpiece clock had been ticking away resolutely while everyone was intent on the game and was now thirty-three minutes shy of chiming the midnight hour.

"The champagne," his fiancée reminded him. "Quick. We need to fill everyone's glass."

"On my way."

He lined up fifteen flute glasses on the drinks cabinet ready to put on a tray, and stoked up the fire.

Some of the guests rose from the coffee table to help themselves to the new spread of snacks Helen was setting out on the buffet table. Drew approached Zoe, who stood at one end fumbling among the heap of handbags. Julie's eyes followed him possessively.

When it became obvious the house agent was chatting up the aspiring young actress and not simply making a comment in passing, she strode purposefully towards the pair. Rex only hoped it wasn't Zoe whom Drew hoped to kiss at the stroke of twelve. A painful scene would be bound to ensue.

5
MURDER IS AFOOT

Rex chatted with John and Alistair for a few minutes. He then loaded a tray with empty glasses and headed, whistling, towards the kitchen to put the champagne on ice. Everything was going grand. The guests seemed to be enjoying themselves. Even Margarita Delacruz was laughing now and talking more freely. He couldn't have devised a better diversion to break the ice than a poem containing clues pointing to hidden treasure. And Julie's party game had livened things up even further. It promised to be a memorable Hogmanay party indeed.

About to set one foot in the kitchen, he stopped in his tracks. Helen and Julie sat in the breakfast nook looking as though someone had died. Julie's mascara had smeared over her cheekbones, her fine blue eyes red and swollen. She clutched a tissue and blew her nose into it when she saw him. Too late to back out now, he thought with regret, taking in the tearful scene and suspecting what it was all about. He recalled too many scenes from his dim and distant past of women crying in kitchens at parties to want to witness this one.

"Sorry to intrude," he said, depositing the tray by the sink. Anything I can do, or should I just get lost?"

"It's Drew," Helen explained needlessly, squeezing her friend's forearm. "He's jilted her."

She's only known him five minutes, Rex was about to protest, stopping himself just in time. The women didn't want to hear reason at such a time. They just wanted to vent.

"Drew likes to play the field," he said. "That's just the way he is."

"How do you know?" Julie asked

with a sob in her throat.

"Just the impression I got in my dealings with him. When we were house-hunting across the Highlands, his phone was constantly going off. He was fielding calls from two or more women. It was rather distracting, in fact. In the end, I got a new agent, though we stayed on friendly terms."

"Drew is too attractive for his own good," Helen remarked.

Rex put the champagne bottles in ice buckets and prepared to make his exit, glancing around to see if there was anything else he needed to take into the living room. Perhaps another log for the fire... He exited the kitchen door leading outside and ventured forth into the bone-chilling night to the woodshed while sleet lashed into his face. A man's shoe prints showed in the slush on the patio. One of the guests must have been back here for some reason, he thought; perhaps for a smoke. He headed in the opposite direction and unlatched the door to the woodshed. It creaked on its hinges as it swung open. Dark and murky, the shed gave out the scent of newly sawn pinewood, and also smelled of cold. He reached towards the neatly stacked cords, grabbed a thick branch, and rushed back to the house, grateful for the warmth of the kitchen.

Helen still sat patiently consoling Julie. He felt he should offer some words of solace himself. "Plenty of fish in the sea, lass," he placated the jilted Julie.

To his consternation, her head sank into her arms on the pine table, and she started to sob uncontrollably. Helen directed him a look that clearly stated, "Now look what you've done!"

He beat a hasty retreat, remembering too late he had forgotten the champagne, and after placing the branch in the log holder, went to confront Drew. "What on earth did you say to Julie?" he said. "She's prostrate on my kitchen table, watering down the meringues."

Drew raised his hands in surrender. "Nothing, I swear! I simply mentioned I was seeing someone in Inverness. She said I'd been leading her on, which, I assure you, is not the case. She's been pursuing me ever since we first met. She thought because I was spending Hogmanay here it must mean something, but I'm here because Heather's in Chicago visiting her sister who's about to have a baby. Must be cold and windy there, much like here tonight." He grimaced in a disarming manner. "Had it been Florida, I might have been persuaded to go." The house agent took a slug of whisky from his tumbler.

"Drew, you unfeeling devil! Well, I've got women wailing in my kitchen thanks to you. And everything was going so well."

"Sorry," Drew said with a hangdog look. "Should I go and apologize?"

"What good would that do?"

"I don't know. I could say I do have feelings for her, just so I don't completely ruin her Hogmanay."

"For goodness sake, Drew, don't be such a numpty. The damage is done."

"Well, I don't know what to say. I never made any promises. We could have had a fun fling, no harm done, even made a few fireworks. She certainly looked ready for it."

Rex did not appreciate this sort of talk. And then he wondered: Had anyone brought fireworks? He'd overlooked that item. Not that it was the weather for them. In any case, fireworks could be dangerous and he didn't want any accidents.

"I think Julie was hoping for more than a fling," he pointed out.

Drew grew cross. "She was leading

me on. And as soon as she saw me talking to Zoe, she stalked over and told me I was a lying cheat. I was only asking Zoe about her acting. I considered being an actor when I was her age. Got a headshot done and went to a few auditions. Eventually did some commercials. But the rejections became demoralizing after a while, and so did not making enough money. It's a competitive business and you've got to know the right people. I just wanted to wish Zoe good luck."

At that moment, Helen joined them and put an arm around Rex. "Oh, what would a New Year's Eve party be without some kitchen drama?" she said brightly. "By the way, I put the champagne over there by the glasses."

"Thanks, lass. Where's Julie?" Rex asked. "It's almost time."

"Fixing her face." Helen glanced at Drew and managed a tight smile. She clearly blamed him.

"A case of mixed signals," Rex explained. "Drew is already spoken for."

"Perhaps something he should have communicated to Julie from the start?" Helen looked pointedly at Drew.

"And I suppose you think I was taking advantage."

"On the face of it, I do," Helen said, never one to mince words even though she always came off sounding reasonable.

"I'm sorry. Really. I know she's a close friend." Drew wandered off, uncertain which direction to take, but avoiding Zoe.

"I hope he's more straightforward with his clients," Helen remarked, piqued for her friend.

"Perhaps you should not have encouraged her," Rex said in Drew's defence.

Helen smiled at him warmly and raised an eyebrow. "I hope we're not going to have a row over it?"

"Definitely not. It's their quarrel. But you best get her back in for the big moment."

Suddenly remembering his elderly guest in the wheelchair, Rex asked Vanessa if they should tell her husband it was time to ring in the New Year.

"No, don't let's wake him. He's sound asleep. This is far beyond his bedtime, poor dear."

Rex thought the cheering at midnight would be bound to wake him anyway, but said nothing. He circulated with the flutes of champagne on a tray and everyone took one, including Julie who smiled at him and said, "Thanks, I really need this." She had managed to compose herself and repair most of the damage to her makeup. She wore a glittery tiara with a pink and silver cardboard sign on top that read, "*Happy Hogmanay!*" He gave her an encouraging wink. Helen, he saw, had donned identical headgear.

Drew, in an effort at chivalry, hovered by Julie's side after accepting his drink and tentatively took her hand. With everyone served, the guests convened in the middle of the room and began the countdown to midnight:

Ten–nine–eight–
HAPPY NEW YEAR!

The clock chimed ceremoniously as the two hands came together in a clap. Exclamations burst forth accompanied by the tooting and squawking of blowouts, some of which played tunes, creating a raucous cacophony. Toasts were made and the champagne was drunk amid an eruption of colourful streamers. Guests embraced their partners in the midst of general good cheer. Rex turned to kiss Helen. Above her head, he noticed Drew crushing lips with Julie and holding her in a tight clinch. Flora and Jason were likewise engaged.

Alistair struck up the opening words of "Auld Lang Syne": *"Should auld acquaintance be forgot,"* and everyone joined in, depositing their empty flute glasses on tables and forming a large circle with arms linked across chests, right hands clasping the left hand of the person to their left. As they sang the Robbie Burn's verses with gusto, moving their linked arms up and down to the rhythm, the storm outside reached a crescendo of its own. A gust of wind rushed down the chimneypiece sending embers from the crumbling white log flurrying onto the stonework in front of the fireplace and blowing out a couple of candles on the coffee table.

With the fire nearly out and the loss of candlelight, the room darkened considerably. Everyone laughed and tried to keep up with the last lines of the chorus. In the grand finale, they all dashed forward, threw their arms up in the air, hands still joined, and turned around to run back in an outer-facing circle, shrieking with laughter and whooping in delight. At that moment, the music and electric chandelier went out, leaving aflame only a few small candles positioned in the outer reaches of the room, which hardly gave any light out at all.

"Oooh, spooky," joked Jason, who was immediately told to hush up by his girlfriend.

"A toppled tree must have snapped the power line," John said.

"Possibly, but we've had heavy snow and never lost power," Rex remarked. "I'll check the fuse box. Helen, do we have any more candles?"

"I think Julie and I used them all."

"There's an oil lamp in the kitchen pantry and matches by the fire. I'll fetch the lamp."

He was heading towards the hall when an exclamation of surprise arose as someone backed into a piece of furniture in the dark and landed with a soft thud. He could discern the shape of a woman in the armchair, but was not sure if it was Vanessa or Catriona. Before he could ask if she was alright, a loud *rap-rap* sounded at the front door.

"Who comes calling on this windy, wintry night?" Cleverly intoned, his sonorous voice unmistakable in the gloom as yet another candle flickered and went out.

"A visitor, so late?" Helen asked in surprise, close enough that Rex could make out the soft contours of her face.

"It's a Scottish custom known as 'first-footing,' whereby friends come calling at midnight with gifts to help welcome in the New Year."

"Not in this weather, surely."

"A tall, dark, handsome stranger is considered the best luck," John said. At least, Rex thought it was John among the several shadows flitting around the living room. "A redheaded woman, the worst."

"Well, is someone going to answer the door, or should we just let them freeze on the doorstep?" Julie demanded.

"I'll go," Cleverly said before Rex could stop him and go himself. "I'm closest."

"Here, take a candle." Rex fetched one by the side window.

The professor's slightly stooped shape retreated around the door and his footsteps shuffled down the hall. Everyone waited in almost complete darkness amid growing anticipation as they listened. In the absence of voices and music, the clock could be heard striking the quarter hour even as the wind outside whipped up a frenzy. Rex heard the front door open. A draught swept down the hallway. There appeared to be an exchange of muted conversation, covered by the wind.

"I hope it is a tall, dark, handsome stranger," Julie remarked. "As tall and handsome as Drew. I'd love to give Mister Harper a taste of his own medicine."

"I wonder why a dark-haired man is considered so lucky. Why not blond?" Helen said.

A few more minutes passed before the front door slammed shut, causing Rex to jump.

"Who is it?" he called out to Cleverly.

"Nobody," the professor called back. His form reappeared in the living room doorway, his face an eerie orb glowing in the candlelight. Rex made his way towards him and took the candle. "I went outside and looked around," Cleverly said. "The climbing vine outside your door was knocking on the wood. There's a gale blowing."

"I thought I heard voices."

"Just the murmur of the wind, I expect."

"I'll get the oil lamp," Rex said. A drop of melted wax dripped onto his hand from the candle.

"Careful, hold it steady," Cleverly warned.

Rex retrieved the lamp from the kitchen pantry and took it to the living room. He lit the lamp wick with a match, replaced the glass cover, and stirred the embers in the fireplace, piling kindling on top and blowing with the bellows. Once he got flames going, he added a small branch from the log holder. A fire leapt to life and he added the large piece of wood from the shed.

Swiping the soot from his hands, he got up from his kneeling position and brushed the fallen embers from his corduroys. Peering closely at Ace Weaver, he saw the old man was fast asleep, his face undoubtedly handsome in youth now slack and crosshatched with deep lines, and his long body broken in his wheelchair. Rex picked up the lamp by its handle and placed it at the centre of the coffee table so that a pool of light radiated from its wick. Like moths drawn to a candle, the guests, stumbling in the outer darkness, drew close and began seating themselves around the table, cheerful and slightly drunk for the most part.

Rex took note of each guest in turn. "Where are Catriona and Ken?" he asked whomever might be listening.

"Catriona passed out on that armchair," Alistair said pointing into the room. She tripped back into it with a gasp and then settled in quite comfortably."

John chortled. "She was tipsy. I saw her fall back and conk oot. It was actually quite funny."

Rex, ever the solicitous host, went to see that she was in fact comfortable and, viewing her peaceful form, draped a throw rug over her lap, since the cold was creeping into the room now that the central heating had gone out. He lit the dead candles and, taking one, proceeded into the hall, almost bumping headlong into Jason who was groping along the walls.

"Have you seen Ken Fraser? Rex asked the student.

"I haven't. He's not in the cloakroom. I've just come from there."

"That's odd. Did he go oot?"

Jason shrugged and continued on his way. Rex continued on his and discovered, to his annoyance, that he could not get the electricity to turn back on. "Blast it," he muttered. He tried again to no avail and shut the small metal door. He called the power company to report the outage and found himself on hold for fifteen minutes. Meanwhile, he could hear voices and laughter coming from the living room. At least his guests were having a good time, but that could not be expected to last once the house got really cold and all the candles and lamp oil ran out.

He reflected on how much firewood he had stockpiled in the shed and calculated there was enough to see them through the night. The bedrooms didn't have wood-burning fireplaces. Perhaps Ken Fraser was tucked up in a bed upstairs? He'd had a lot to drink, so anything was possible. That would certainly be better than him lying outside drunk or hurt somewhere. Rex wished he had enough light to properly explore the lodge inside and out.

"Hello, hello?" he said into the phone, hearing a click, but, no, he was still on hold.

Fortunately, he had a refurbished vintage AGA that ran on gas, and they would be able to heat up the soup Helen had prepared. The stove gave out heat as well, so at least the kitchen would be a bearable temperature. And he had plenty of blankets. The guests could camp out on the living room sofas and armchairs until the alcohol wore off and they felt able to drive home. Coffee. How could they make coffee? He'd think of something even if it was only the instant kind.

"Yes? Hullo!" Finally. He explained his dilemma to a sympathetic female voice of the Highlands and, at the end of the call, after a quick check of the downstairs rooms, returned to the living room and enquired whether Ken had turned up yet. He had not, and no one appeared unduly concerned.

"No luck with the electricity," he informed the quests. "But I reported it." He hesitated a moment. "I'm going to look ootside for Ken," he said.

"He won't be out there," Alistair remonstrated. "You'll freeze to death, dear man."

"Well, he must be somewhere,"

Vanessa said. "He'd not have disappeared into thin air, would he?"

"He might have gone to fetch something from his car and slipped on ice. Anything might have happened."

Rex knew this to his cost, something dreadful having happened at the lodge in more clement weather.

"I'll go with you," Alistair volunteered with a deep sigh. "John?"

The medic cursed under his breath. "Fine, but let's check the other rooms first. He may have wanted to find a quiet place to curl up in and nurse a hangover."

"Aye, I thought of that. I looked downstairs."

"If he's not upstairs, John and I will certainly help you search for that pompous ass," Alistair repeated his offer.

"Me too," Drew said, rising from the loveseat to Julie's obvious consternation. She clamped shut her lips and folded her arms above the blanket that had covered both their laps.

"Can I do anything?" Helen asked Rex with concern.

"If you could heat up that beef and barley soup and maybe some bread rolls, that would be grand."

Flora offered to help and rose from the sofa, pulling her blue mohair shawl tighter around her shoulders.

"Good," Jason said. "I was beginning to get peckish again."

"Leave some for us," John pleaded, "while we go brave the elements."

"I should go with you." Jason spoke with detectable reluctance.

"Just sit tight, mate, and take care of the ladies."

"I can do that." The student put a friendly arm around Zoe, a stupid grin plastered over his face.

The young actress giggled and shrugged him away. "Get off me, you big lump!"

Jason moved over to where Vanessa Weaver was seated and did the same with her. She laughed. "Don't let my husband catch you. He was lethal in his youth, you know. His plane went down in enemy territory and he had to fight his way out, killing half a dozen Germans." However, she seemed content enough to have the young man's arm around her, clearly enjoying the attention. Rex thought Jason probably wouldn't risk a similar manoeuvre with Señora Delacruz. He might get a slap in the face.

While Helen, Julie and Flora busied themselves in the kitchen, the men convened in the hall, discussing how best to organize the search, the objective being to cover as much ground as possible in the least amount of time. They started putting on their coats and anoraks, all but Rex who took a candle and climbed upstairs to look there first. The floorboards creaked more than usual and bumps sounded from the attic. He checked all four bedrooms and the two bathrooms. Ken was nowhere to be found.

He brought down extra layers and gloves for the search, as well as the electric torch he kept by the bed. He gave it to John while he donned the additional clothing.

"I have a more powerful torch in my car," Alistair said.

"Good, we'll need it."

When Rex opened the front door, sleet flew in his face, stinging his eyes. Cautiously, he walked into the courtyard and looked about him. Black ice and wet gravel glinted among the guests' vehicles. The station wagon belonging to the Weavers stood closest to the front door, the Frasers' dark blue sedan just beyond it. Alistair's silver Porsche, then Drew's white BMW, the professor's Morris Minor, and the students' old jalopy were positioned in receding order of arrival. Helen's Renault and his own Mini Cooper were parked in the old stables that had been converted into a garage. The exposed area of driveway was crisscrossed with tire tracks, the snow fluted at the edges like pastry crust where he had cleared it that afternoon.

The biting cold served to wake him up even as his extremities went numb. How much he would have preferred not to have been out on this particular night looking for an errant guest! The wind chill made the experience all the more miserable, and he felt rotten about having to subject three of his guests to the unpleasant task, especially as there was no knowing what they might find.

6
A GRIM FIND

On the steep, wooded hillside around him loomed dark Scots pines, dripping birch trees and junipers. Ghostly contrails of mist floated among the tall trunks. The moon was barely visible through the glowering clouds, casting the lodge and outbuildings in dense shadow, the front door under the stone porch a solid black rectangle. Had the electricity been on, the mysterious caller might have rung the bell—unless nobody had been outside to begin with. The wind was rapping the branches of the overgrown vine against the door, but not as loudly now. The gale seemed to be dying down.

Alistair and John had diverged to search the stables and the back of the house and loch. Rex shivered to think of the wind-rippled wavelets in the grey lake. No one in Ken's state could survive the chill of the water for long. Alistair, who had taken his powerful light, re-joined him with a hopeless shrug of the shoulders. He played his beam around the recesses of the courtyard and between the parked cars. Diamond crystals glinted in the orb of his light on the ground sheened with frost at their feet.

"No sign of Ken in the stables or meadow," he reported, his breath fogging in the cold air. "I searched every nook and cranny. What's a cranny, anyway? Sod this sleet," he cursed, swiping at his eyes with a gloved hand.

John came up shortly afterward, shaking his head ensconced in a black beanie hat. "I don't think he's oot here. If he is, I hate to think what state he'll be in, especially if he went into the loch. I couldn't see far because of the mist." The medic clutched his mitted hands together for warmth.

"Perhaps we should all three search the loch and walk a short way up the shore," Rex suggested. "Just to be certain. Where's Drew?"

"He stayed behind to explore the house first, the canny beggar," John said, clearly miffed.

"He's taking his sweet time about it," Alistair remarked.

The men moved off in the direction of the loch.

"I've found him!" Drew yelled from the front door. "He's in the broom cupboard. He must have crawled in there to keep warm."

"Is he okay?" Rex demanded, turning back, gruff from anxiety and cold, but relieved they would not have to search by the open loch, fully exposed to the wind.

"I cannot tell. I think he's unconscious. Perhaps John should come and take a look."

The trio trooped back inside the

lodge, stamping the slush off their boots and shoes on the mat. Rex divested himself of his anorak while John approached Drew standing outside the broom closet. Rex took stock. Located opposite the blank wall of the living room, whose door was further down the hall, the closet was not visible to anyone in the room, unless they were positioned in the doorway. The house agent stepped aside for John who held the light Rex had given him.

"This is the last place I looked," Drew said.

There was little room in the closet beneath the stairs, which housed mops and a vacuum cleaner, or Rex would have thought to look in it. As it was, he could see Ken Fraser in a comatose stupor slumped up against the far wall with his knees to his chest, before John's crouching body hid him entirely from view. After a few minutes, the medic backed out of the space and turned a concerned look upon the three men waiting for news.

"He's not breathing. No pulse. I closed his eyes. I'm afraid he's gone."

"Dead?" Alistair asked in shock. "Are you sure?"

"Course I'm sure."

"Was it the booze?" Drew asked. "Alcohol poisoning or something?"

"Possibly. It would be better if I could examine him properly. But we need to get an ambulance here at once just to be safe."

Alistair got on his phone while Rex made arrangements to take Ken into the living room. He called Helen from the doorway and asked her to cover the sofa by the side window.

"We have a body," he explained. "We found Ken Fraser in the broom cupboard."

Helen gasped, clamping a hand to her mouth. "Dead?" she finally managed to ask, echoing Alistair.

"Think so, but we don't know how he died. John and Drew are bringing him oot now."

She tore the festive tiara from her abundant blond hair. "I can't believe this," she said on the verge of tears.

He took her in his arms and kissed the top of her head. "I know, lass. And tonight of all nights." Or any night, for that matter.

"Well," she said wiping away an incipient tear. "We had better just deal with it. It's not like we haven't before."

"Helen," he said, cupping her chin and lifting her face to his. "Just when I think I couldn't love you any more, I find that I do."

Her bottom lip trembled, but she managed a smile. "I suppose I'd better get a sheet and whatnot." She hurried up the stairs to the armoire on the landing. He regretted putting her through such a situation again, and marvelled at how she always came up trumps.

He entered the living room and tried to rouse Catriona in her armchair. Her eyes were closed, and she did not respond. He dreaded having to inform her that her husband was in all likelihood dead. He shook her more forcefully and repeated her name. Her head lolled to one side, her greying auburn hair falling over her face.

"John," he shouted hoarsely.

Drew and the medic were laying Ken's body on the sofa as Alistair and Helen stood by in silence.

"What's the matter?" John asked approaching.

"You had better check Catriona. She's not showing any signs of life either."

John swore abruptly and flew to her side. The other guests were beginning to ask questions from where they sat around the fireplace. They probably thought Ken was sleeping and the others were simply making him more comfortable. Rex told them he would explain in a minute and to keep their seats in the meantime. He heard some questioning murmurs of concern, but his attention was now directed to something puzzling as he looked over at Ken. He was sure the grey-and-white scarf around his neck had been loose during the course of the night, but now it was knotted securely. Perhaps Ken had grown cold inside the closet and tightened it.

Acting on a hunch, Rex went over to the body and, bending over, untied the scarf. On the left side of Ken's neck, he noticed a small puncture wound oozing blood. A lot more had been absorbed by the scarf. Upon closer inspection, he saw the hole contained a sticky dark brown residue.

"What the heck," Alistair began beside him, peering at the man's neck with the aid of his torch. "What is that?"

"I don't know. Best call the police."

"She's dead," John announced from halfway across the room.

"Did you see this when you were checking his vitals?" Rex asked the medic now standing beside him.

"No. I just reached inside the scarf to check his pulse. That looks like a wound made by a knifepoint. It's almost completely round. Look, here's his pipe," John said pulling the object from the dead man's trouser pocket. "Stone cold. What happened here?"

"Damned if I know," Alistair said. "It couldn't be a snake bite or something, could it?"

The only poisonous snakes in Scotland were adders, but not in winter, and not in one's home, Rex thought. Mostly, one saw them around boulders out on the moorland in summer and in the spring.

"You'd expect to find two

perforations from a snake, and I only see one. And the location on the body is unlikely," John said.

"Especially if it was covered up with the scarf." Rex straightened to his full height and asked, "Did you see something similar on Catriona?"

"I didn't notice anything." John went back to the armchair, and Rex followed. The medic examined Mrs. Fraser's neck, moving her hair away on each side and at the back. There were no similar marks. Nor anywhere else on her exposed skin, which was limited to her neck, face, and hands. She wore stockings in her shoes beneath the dove-grey satin pantsuit.

At that moment, Vanessa Weaver spoke behind Rex, jolting him from his disturbing reflections.

"I'm sorry. What did you say?" he asked.

"I said, 'What on earth is going on?' You keep examining the Frasers like they were dolls."

"Dead bodies," John corrected. "Something strange is going on, Vanessa. And until we find oot what it is, we could all be in danger."

Vanessa cried out, hands flying to her throat.

Rex stared in surprise at the young man. "Where's your bedside manner, John? No need to frighten everybody more than is absolutely necessary."

"She needs to stay away unless she can be of assistance," the medic said shortly. "I'm trying to think what could have killed this woman." He looked over Catriona's neck and throat again.

"The plaster on her thumb," Rex said of a sudden. "Check there."

The medic did so, unpeeling it. It had lost some of its adhesiveness. "Aye, look here," he told Rex. "The cut is deep and round. Quite a bit of blood. Don't know how we missed it. Some has escaped the plaster."

"It's dark. Excuse me, Vanessa." Rex gently moved the interior designer aside. "Hm, the cut is deeper than she received from the glass, I'll warrant."

"But not as deep a wound as on Ken," John said peering at the victim's thumb with the torch. "I hope I haven't disturbed any evidence if this is a crime." He glanced up at Rex. "Well, I suppose it must be, right? What caused the roundish wounds on the bodies, I cannot say, but something pointed, obviously."

"What are you talking about?" Mrs. Weaver demanded.

"Vanessa, do you mind sitting back down and trying to keep the guests calm?" Rex asked. "I'll be over once I know a bit more."

She went reluctantly and was immediately besieged by questions from the other guests. Rex tried to tune them out. He pinched his eyes shut and tried to think clearly.

"Is there dark stuff in the blood?" he asked John.

"Aye, in the wound. Darker than dried blood. What is it? It's not powder."

"Perhaps we should check the old gentleman and make sure he's not dead too."

John made his way over to the wheelchair by the fire. "Sleeping soundly," he reported. "Regular, if wheezy, breathing and pulse. I don't suppose he's a suspect?" the medic asked in an attempt at levity when he re-joined Rex.

"Well, if he is, he's far down the list. But perhaps he heard or saw something the rest of us didn't."

"Unlikely. His chair is facing into the corner."

"Wheelchairs are moveable."

"His is an old-fashioned one

without much mobility beyond forward and backward propulsion. When he wakes up, I'll tell him he can hopefully get an electric one on the NHS."

"I don't know how much time he spends in it," Rex said. "I'll have to ask Vanessa."

"Quite a bit, I suspect. His arms are strong for his age. I noticed that when I helped him into his chair when we arrived. Pushing yourself around in one of those manual wheelchairs will build up your muscles."

Alistair came and put an arm around John. "You can look after me in my dotage."

"And I thought you were only after my body," the young medic quipped.

No doubt John's flippancy derived from having seen too many casualties from traffic accidents and other everyday tragedies. Alistair, like Rex, a prosecutor of the most heinous crimes, was accustomed to death in all its forms too. However, it was worse when the deceased were guests at your party.

Rex excused himself and went to build up the fire before he addressed the remaining guests. As he worked, he wondered who could have crept up to Catriona's armchair and pricked her thumb as she slept in a drink-induced slumber. Had she gasped from surprise or pain before collapsing in the chair? How long had she been dead and not asleep at all? And who had closed her eyes? It was all rather sinister.

"Of course, everybody's horribly upset over the Frasers' passing," Helen commented when he had finished with the fire. "But they're not panicking, fortunately."

"The Frasers did not 'pass,' lass," he said in a low voice. "They were murdered. 'Passing' implies some passive event befalling them, like death from natural causes, whereas evidence suggests someone was very active in their demise."

"Don't quibble, Rex. Not now. What I mean is the guests are holding up pretty well under the circumstances."

"They're in shock, and they probably think, if it was murder, the killer came in from the cold, so to speak. And that this intruder has since disappeared, having achieved his objective."

"What would that be?"

"That of killing the Fraser couple, no doubt for monetary gain or revenge."

"But you don't think so?"

Rex led Helen aside, out of earshot. "I think it likely at least one of our guests is not concerned aboot anything except getting caught."

Helen drew in a sharp breath. "And who might that be?" It was getting cold in the room away from the fire, and she huddled in her cardigan. No doubt fear had something to do with the gesture as well.

"I honestly don't have a clue at this point."

"But it could be an intruder all the same," Helen persisted, naturally preferring the alternative of a stranger who had long since disappeared from the property. "After all, we wouldn't have heard a vehicle in the storm. A four-wheel drive would have managed the slope without too much trouble. Did you venture out far enough to see if there were any new tracks? Or they could have left the vehicle at the top of the hill and walked down through the trees. The knock at the door could have been a ruse while the culprit ran to the kitchen door and came in that way. Perhaps he hid in the broom cupboard."

"Aye, the kitchen door was unlocked. I'll go and bolt it, though it's a wee bit late now." It was then he remembered the footprints in the slush.

When was it he had gone out to fetch wood? It had to have been before midnight since he was about to get the champagne.

"He could have come upon Ken wandering about in the dark," Helen said. "And then sneaked into the living room and killed Catriona in her chair while you were on the phone to the power company."

"I was at the end of the hall for a quarter of an hour. I would have seen someone leave the kitchen."

"Well, before, then. Or else he came in through the window in here. It was slightly ajar before I closed it."

"When did you do that?"

"While you were all out looking for Ken. It was getting cold. And it was dark. What if he's still in the house?"

"I think someone would have noticed a draught or some noise if someone climbed in. Having said that, I will of course inform the police about the open window and unlocked door."

Helen's lips twitched in a wry smile. "Of course you will, Rex. You want them to spend time on a wild goose chase while you solve the crime on your own."

"Helen! I am duty bound to apprise law enforcement of all pertinent facts, which I fully expect them to explore while, as you say, I pursue my own lines of enquiry."

With a complicit wink, he called 9-9-9 to report two suspicious deaths at Gleneagle Lodge, his doomed second home and country retreat. For the first time since acquiring the property, he thought about selling it.

He explained to the dispatcher that a call had already been put through for an ambulance, but there was now no question the two victims were dead. He confirmed directions to the lodge. "Aye, between Invergarry and Laggan, north of the swing bridge. Also, we have no power. We're making do with torches and candles, and one oil lamp. Please inform the police of that fact."

It was one-thirty in the morning on the first day of January and not an auspicious start to the year.

7
TO CATCH A KILLER

The guests sat anxiously waiting for Rex to explain the meaning of the two dead bodies in the living room. Rex mulled over what to say. Alistair, John and Drew stood on the periphery of the group, as though in a separate camp from those who had not been party to the discovery of Ken Fraser in the broom closet and the subsequent realization that his wife had met a similar end.

Rex cleared his throat as he faced his guests, those with their backs to him at the coffee table turning around in their seats. Eight numb expressions faced him in the light of the oil lamp and candles, the professor's spectacles reflecting flames off their spheres. Vanessa had turned her husband's wheelchair towards Rex, but the old man was in shadow and Rex could not determine whether or not he was awake.

"As you are all aware, the unthinkable has happened," Rex announced. "Ken and Catriona Fraser are dead, and I won't beat aboot the bush: They were most likely murdered."

Gasps and sobs erupted, although the news could have come as no surprise, since Vanessa would have told them what she knew. Margarita Delacruz, sitting straight and solemn, crossed herself and kissed a silver necklace she wore under her dress, murmuring something in Spanish.

"We don't yet know exactly how, and we don't know by whom," Rex continued. "Now, without wishing to alarm you, we must assume, just to err on the side of caution, that the perpetrator is among us."

This suggestion elicited a chorus of protests and objections. Rex ignored them. "It is, of course, possible that someone entered the house without our knowledge and committed the crimes for whatever reason, but that, to my mind, is a less likely scenario, pending further evidence. Naturally, the police have been alerted and will be here shortly. I suggest we all stay put and remain patient. In the meantime, if anyone has any relevant information or suspicions, I would be glad to hear it. If we can facilitate proceedings, the police will be finished with us sooner, and we can all go home."

He wanted Helen and Julie back in Edinburgh at the earliest opportunity. A person who had killed twice wouldn't hesitate to kill again.

"Do you think this has anything to do with the previous murder at Gleneagle Lodge?" Flora inevitably asked, with a catch in her voice.

"I don't at this point, quite honestly," Rex said. "That killer was caught and I don't see a connection to the Frasers."

"I wonder why they were targeted," Vanessa Weaver remarked. "They were very unassuming people. But what if it was random?" She shuddered at this possibility.

"God, I hope there won't be a lot of publicity," Zoe exclaimed. "I don't want to sound selfish, but it might ruin my chances with the audition." She looked positively put out and cast a look of blame at Rex.

"Some thoughts are better kept to oneself, Zoe," her mother chided. "No one wants to be associated with murder, but we must do whatever we can to help."

"Thank you, Vanessa."

"But I did try to warn you, Rex. Thirteen guests, you know."

Well, eleven now, by your calculations, Rex thought, irritated by her senseless remarks. And perhaps still counting...

"Ehm," began Jason, squeezing Flora's hand, "Are you sure they're dead and not just unconscious? I've been to loads of student parties where people get smashed out of their brains and pass out, and don't surface for hours."

"John is quite sure. He is a paramedic, after all."

"Aye, I forgot." Jason rubbed at his brow. "But did they die of too much alcohol? You must have some idea."

Rex turned to John, offering him the floor.

"We found small entry wounds in their bodies," the medic explained. "Small and quite neat. I'm not sure I've ever seen anything like this even during training. I mean, I studied snake bites, and if there'd been a pair of holes, I might have thought something like that. But that wouldn't make sense anyway in the dead of winter."

"Holes, like from a jab?" Zoe asked.

"I would say so. But a jab alone would not have caused death in the places they were found."

"And where was that?" the señora inquired.

"In Ken Fraser's neck, not in an artery or major vessel, and in his wife's thumb."

"Her thumb!" Julie exclaimed. "Where she cut herself on the glass?"

John nodded, tight-lipped.

"Could she have got an infection from the glass?"

The medic shook his head. "Don't think so. And then there's her husband's wound, similar but deeper. And more blood."

Flora made a gagging motion and put a hand to her mouth. Rex hoped she was not going to be sick, and was about to go to her aid when she appeared to recover and smiled reassuringly at Jason, who was also watching her with concern.

"And in each case the wound was hidden," John added gravely. "By Ken's scarf and Catriona's plaster."

"Which makes it all the more suspicious," Vanessa contributed to the discussion.

"Wait! Now I get it," Zoe burst out. "It's another game, isn't it?" She pointed to Rex, Alistair, John, and Drew. "They plotted it when they were talking in the hall. Ken is just pretending to be dead and Catriona is still asleep!" She fell back in her seat laughing.

"Is this true?" Vanessa asked, looking confused and turning to Rex.

"I assure you this is no game."

"If it is, it's in very poor taste," Margarita Delacruz remarked.

Helen threw up her hands. "Rex wouldn't stage something like this. Nor would Alistair. I'm sure John and Drew wouldn't either."

"Perhaps we should be searching for the weapon," Drew Harper said from where he stood beside Alistair. The house agent looked pale and drawn, showing his forty-odd years.

"The police will take care of that," Julie replied tartly. Evidently, she didn't care for the fact that Drew had not returned to comfort her. Helen took hold of her hand and squeezed it.

"I just can't stand this waiting around." His hands in his suit pockets, Drew shifted his weight from one foot to the other. "The police might be held up. It's the worst night of the year for crime and accidents, and the icy weather won't help. Dammit!" He banged his fists into his forehead, possibly wishing he had gone with his lady friend to Chicago, after all.

Rex was of similar mind with regard to searching for the weapon, but was glad not to have been the first to suggest it.

"What if the killer strikes again?" Jason said ominously, causing Flora to sink against his shoulder. The poor girl had already been through enough drama at the lodge to last a lifetime.

"I don't think it's one of us," Vanessa countered, squaring her shoulders and tossing back her red mass of hair in defiance. "I mean, who among us..." Her encompassing glance paused on Margarita and quickly moved on. "It's unthinkable."

"I agree," Cleverly said. "Preposterous. We don't really know what happened. In fact, we know nothing much at all except that two people are dead."

"It could have been something that happened prior," Zoe said, eying the men warily as though they just might be prolonging the charade at everyone else's expense. "Like some weird flesh-eating bacteria the Frasers caught from somewhere." She looked over at John, who looked unconvinced, but said nothing. "Why doesn't someone research it online?"

"I did," said Alistair. "On my phone."

"And?" Zoe asked.

"Nothing very useful came up. I think we had better stick with the facts."

"Spoken like a true prosecutor," John said with a brief smile.

Rex considered the options. The police might arrive immediately, or they might be delayed. In the meantime, he had a dozen anxious people waiting in his living room, one of whom might be anxious for a different reason. He wanted to catch the killer, or at the very least rattle that person enough for them to slip up and give themselves away by word or action.

"Well," he took up again. "Let's make ourselves useful and try to think of what might have caused the wounds to Ken and Catriona Fraser."

"You seriously expect us to sit here calm as can be in the possible presence of a killer?" Margarita Delacruz enquired with haughty distain.

"I'm afraid we don't have much choice," Rex replied. "And let's everybody keep hands where we can see them."

He had a quiet word with Alistair and then started clearing up the soup bowls and plates on the table. Helen rose to help him as did Julie, but Rex told the latter to stay warm by the fire. Drew came over and took Helen's place, to Julie's obvious satisfaction. Alistair and John slid into vacant armchairs, preparing for a bout of brainstorming, while Rex took the loaded tray to the kitchen, Helen in tow with the oil lamp.

He deposited the tray and informed her of his plan to search the guests.

"What if somebody objects?"

"That could be construed as an indication of guilt."

"What if the culprit already disposed of the weapon?"

"It's possible," Rex said. "But they might be keeping it on their person for now."

"In that case, we need to watch everybody before they can get rid of it. That means escorting everyone to the bathroom. Our guests will feel they are under suspicion."

"Well, they are. We could pair them with people we trust. Alistair, for instance."

"And Julie," Helen said.

"And Flora."

"Yes, I don't see her being involved. But Jason? He's a bit of a prankster, isn't he? And that business with the metal detector and not telling anyone he'd found a valuable gold coin."

"But other of our guests have behaved suspiciously. Señora Delacruz is a dark horse. Zoe was rummaging among the handbags. I wonder..."

Helen unloaded the crockery from the tray by the light of the oil lamp. "We don't know exactly when Ken Fraser left the room, but he was with us for 'Auld Lang Syne,' and he never reappeared after the mysterious visitor called."

"Aye," Rex said. "The mysterious visitor."

The one who had not made an appearance.

8
FLYING DEATH

Finding upon their return to the living room that no headway had been made at the guests' end, Rex asked the men, under Alistair's supervision, to turn out their pockets and the women the contents of their handbags, unless they had any objections. None did, or made it apparent that they did.

They should bring in the coats from the hall as well, he said, in case any weapon was concealed in one of them. Still receiving no opposition, Helen piled the ladies' bags on the coffee table.

Flora pointed to hers, a lacy cream affair stitched with fake pearls. "Be my guest," she told Rex.

He snapped on a pair of transparent latex gloves from under the kitchen sink that Helen used for cleaning. They were a tight fit, but he didn't want to compromise any evidence in the event some was found. The police would not appreciate his interference as it was, but time was of the essence. The killer might strike again.

Inside the reticule were Flora's laminated student identity card, a purse, a smartphone, a brush, and a tube of mascara, which Rex untwisted with her permission, only to find that it was indeed a tube of mascara, containing a wand whose tip was coated with black makeup. He felt a trifle silly holding it up in his beefy hand, and the younger women giggled.

"Sorry," Zoe said. "I expect it's nerves. I always want to giggle when I get stage fright."

"Put something on," her mother scolded. "You've got goose bumps all over your arms. It's making me cold just looking at you."

"I'm fine, Mum. Don't fuss!"

In his notebook Rex compiled a list

of the bag's contents under Flora's name and returned everything with his thanks.

"Zoe, is this yours?" he asked, picking up a green leather bag that matched her filmy dress and strappy sandals. She nodded, and he asked her permission to go through it, to which she shrugged in resignation. As the other guests looked on, he upended the bag onto the table and shook it. A compact, a lipstick in the unfortunately designated shade of Killer Red, and an ornate silver money-clip spilled out, along with some loose change and a small packet of spearmint gum. Also, a green velvet ribbon. Rex made an inventory of the items. People started to yawn in the late hour.

"Thank you, Zoe," he said, carefully replacing everything once he had checked there were no inside pockets.

Zoe retrieved her bag and clutched

it protectively to her chest. Alistair, directing the men's operations, went from guest to guest patting down pockets, first Cleverly's, then Drew's, turning up nothing of interest, mainly wallets, keys, and an assortment of phones.

Rex took hold of the next evening bag that came to hand. "And whose is this?" he asked.

"Mine," said Vanessa.

Murmuring his apologies, he unfastened the gold clasp and emptied the contents, which were similar in substance to her daughter's but more expensive, and included a tin of cough drops instead of chewing gum. A curious object dropped out from among the clutter. At first he thought it was a fly fishing lure, such as he kept under lock and key in his study at the lodge.

"Oh, I forgot about this," Vanessa said, picking it up off the table before Rex could prevent her. "Did anyone here lose it? I found it on the floor." She looked expectantly around the table. Alistair had suspended his search and was gazing at the pointed, feathery-tailed object in her hand.

"What is it?" Julie asked. "Did it come off a dress?"

"At first I thought it was from an earring," Vanessa explained. "Rather exotic, I thought. I assumed it belonged to Margarita, and then I saw she was wearing amber stones." She looked at the woman's ears to make sure. The señora averted her dark eyes. "I suppose I thought it was hers because it matches her black sequined bag with the tassels, but I never got the opportunity to give it to her. Now I'm not so sure it is an earring."

She held it out at arm's length to the oil lamp and peered at the small tuft of shiny black feathers. "I need my reading glasses. Ace, love?" When she saw her non-responsive husband was dozing, she muttered, "Oh, never mind. We share a pair," she explained. "He keeps them on him so I don't lose them, which I'm prone to do."

"Let me see," said Zoe leaning in beside her. "Oh, look. It's got some yucky stuff on the tip. What is it?" she asked, drawing back her hand in disgust.

Rex reached over. "May I?" he asked, taking the object from Vanessa. "Hm. Looks like a small dart with the feathers forming the fletch."

"A dart," Alistair repeated.

"Wait a minute..." John said, without finishing his sentence, his face expressing a sudden revelation.

"It's tiny," Julie said. "Are you sure it's a dart?"

Rex held it back to the light. "But still potentially lethal if poisoned. That might account for the dark sticky residue on its point, similar to that found in the wounds." He showed the object to John, who nodded.

Everyone reacted with shock to the idea of poison.

"I may have touched it!" Vanessa cried.

"Could be poison," Professor Cleverly agreed, craning his neck to better see the item in question. "But," he added, dismissing Mrs. Weaver's fears with a wave of his long-tapered fingers, "if it's curare, as it might be, judging by the colour and consistency, it's not harmful if you touch it, unless you have a cut or abrasion."

A cut or abrasion, Rex repeated to himself.

"What is curare?" John asked.

"An arrow poison made from tree bark and sometimes mixed with venom," Cleverly told him. "Used by tribes in tropical South America to hunt monkeys and other small game, and known as 'flying death'."

"They really eat monkeys?" Jason

exclaimed. "I've never tried monkey meat."

"Come off it, everybody," Drew objected, throwing up his hands. "Who would bring a poison dart to a party?"

The murderer, Rex thought. And where was the other dart? One for each victim, presumably. Were there others? His blood ran cold at the thought.

"Are you sure that's what was used on the Frasers?" Flora asked, straining to take a closer look at the exhibit.

"The point is the right size for the wounds we found," Rex said. "What do you think, John?"

"Aye, and the brownish substance matches."

"It's diabolical," Helen exclaimed. "Who would want to murder such a nice couple?"

"Perhaps it has something to do with the gold they were boasting about." Margarita Delacruz shook her head back in a haughty manner. "Very foolish of them, I think."

Vanessa Weaver concurred. "Oh, I know! Especially as it's just lying up there in the castle. And from what I understood earlier, the gold's been cursed since the beginning and has destroyed the family down through generations. And now this." She looked pointedly at Rex, as though to remind him of her warnings.

Flora turned to her boyfriend. "I think you should get rid of that coin, Jason. Just turn it in to wherever Drew said."

"You'll have to tell the police now," the house agent told him. "If they ever get here," he added, glancing at the mantelpiece clock, which was about to chime two in the morning.

Jason put his hands to his face and nodded. "Bloody hell. I can't believe this. It's like a bad dream."

"I know, lad," Rex said. "But don't blame yourself. You didn't know the story when you found that gold piece."

"I should have known it might be part of the Arkaig Treasure. I did some research when I found it, to determine its value. I thought it might be a stray coin from those times, not part of something bigger."

"We don't know that for sure," Alistair said. "There may be nothing buried at the castle."

"Let's forget the gold for now and find out who shot that thing." Zoe pointed at the dart in Rex's palm, as her mother put a consoling arm around her.

"Wouldn't the dart need a bow or something?" Flora asked. "Or are those only for arrows?"

"Perhaps we should do just that," Rex agreed with Zoe. "And that's a very good point, Flora. There may well be another part to this missile. Humphrey, what was used to launch these darts in the tropics?"

"Blowpipes. They're still in use by the indigenous peoples of South East Asia and South and Central America. They literally blow these darts through pipes. The longer the pipe, the greater the force and subsequent distance."

"Are they accurate?" Rex asked.

"I expect so, since their survival can depend on them. And they're virtually soundless. Have you ever come upon these darts on your travels?" Cleverly asked his female companion.

Everyone listened attentively for the answer, trying not to look too obvious.

"I have not," Margarita stated.

"What are the pipes made of?" Rex enquired of the professor.

"Bamboo, I believe."

"But you could use any material, right?" Jason queried. "A metal tube, or hollowed-out anything."

"I remember a murder mystery

film where a clay pipe was featured," Helen said. "At least, I think it was clay. It wasn't very long. About five inches or so, and it had colourful designs on it."

"That seems a bit short," the professor contended. "The blowpipes used in Borneo are about two metres, longer than the shooter."

"In primary school, we used straws to blow spit wads at our teachers," Jason said. "Same principle as peashooters."

"I bet you were the worst offender," Flora remarked.

"What do you mean? I was the best!"

"I don't think we have any straws here," Rex said.

"Wouldn't it depend on the distance required for the target?" John asked no one in particular. "Blowpipes are used to shoot tranquillizer darts into dangerous animals from a safe distance. I saw that on a television documentary."

"Where on the floor did you find this?" Rex asked Vanessa.

"By Catriona's chair when you and John were examining her. I had dropped my cracker and stooped to pick it up, thinking the cream cheese might make a mess on your rug. The olive had rolled under the chair behind the claw foot. That's where I found that—that thing! I cleaned up the cheese with my paper napkin," she hastened to add, although Rex barely heard her apology, so engrossed was he in the find, inspecting it from every angle. It was a highly curious object, the like of which he had never seen.

"Well done, Vanessa," he said. "We might never have found it so soon otherwise. It's too dark."

"What now?" Alistair enquired. "If we don't believe Vanessa shot the dart..."

"Of course I didn't!" she

remonstrated. "I didn't even know what it was."

"It may have fallen after it pierced Catriona's thumb," John said. "Perhaps it got kicked under the chair, accidentally or otherwise. It was pitch black in the middle of the room when she collapsed, remember. Perhaps the person who shot her couldn't find the object. I don't see how it could have been shot into her, though. For one thing, the plaster over the point of entry is intact."

"It must have been removed and replaced," Alistair said. "The dart might not have been shot at all, just stabbed into her at close range."

Vanessa let out a small scream and Margarita kissed the silver cross at her throat. Rex apologized for upsetting them and decided to pursue the investigation more privately. The last thing he needed was hysteria. In any case, no one seemed able or willing to shed further light on the blow-dart or the circumstances under which it might have been used. Perhaps he might be lucky enough to find the dart that killed Ken Fraser as well, if, in fact, there were two.

To that end, he undertook a careful search of the hall and broom closet with the aid of Alistair's powerful torch. His colleague conducted a broader search. Both men came up empty-handed.

"Back to searching the guests' coats and bags?" Alistair asked.

"I need to reflect a little first based on what we've discovered."

Rex returned to the living room and told his guests he would prepare some coffee and to sit tight until the police arrived. None of them, however, appeared to wish to stray away from the light.

"Curare wasn't the poison used in the film *Death in the Clouds*," Helen told him when they had closed themselves in the kitchen. "I saw it quite recently. I'm sure I'd have remembered that name."

Rex filled the kettle and put it on the red-enamelled AGA, which was still warm from the soup Helen had reheated and which kept the room at a tolerable temperature.

"Margarita's from South America, isn't she?" Helen went on. "She said she liked travelling and sight-seeing. You should ask her about the dart in private. I know she denied knowing anything about them, but she may be hiding something."

"Right. Obviously, we need to discover who brought the dart to the party and why. Looks like this was pre-meditated, but we need a motive."

"The blackout provided the opportunity."

"True. And we also need to find out the means. How were the darts administered?" Rex rummaged in the pantry. "Is there more instant coffee?" Helen opened a cabinet and pulled out a large canister of coffee granules. "Good, I feel it's going to be a long night. How are you holding up, lass?"

"Okay. I'm glad I was able to take a nap this afternoon." Helen prepared the coffee in a large pot. "I still can't believe it. Why at your party? And on New Year's Eve of all nights!"

"Safety in numbers? Inebriation and distraction? I wish I knew."

"Can we rule out John as a suspect?" Helen asked.

"Possibly. But for a medical professional, he did seem a bit slow to respond to the Frasers."

"He probably thought, like the rest of us, that they'd drunk too much and passed out. But he was quick to respond when Drew choked on that chocolate. After that, he probably didn't expect another mishap."

"Mishap?"

"Well, okay, murder. Murders," she corrected herself. "Why do so many happen when you're around? I have often asked myself that question."

"They might go undetected otherwise," Rex replied with an impudent grin. "You'd be surprised how many murders go undetected or unproved."

"Forget I asked."

"He also didn't appear to be well up on poisons," Rex continued on the topic of John.

"He's an ambulance man, Rex. He's not a toxicology expert."

Rex conceded with a grudging nod. "Had Humphrey not been here, we wouldn't know it was curare, if that's what it is."

"I hope it is, for Vanessa's sake. He said it wasn't fatal if it didn't get in your bloodstream. Lucky he knows his anthropology."

"It'd be luckier if none of this had happened at all," Rex remarked.

At that moment, Alistair knocked and entered the kitchen. "Any progress with your deductions, Sherlock?"

"Not really. We were saying earlier that, as one of the non-suspects, you should keep an eye on the others."

"In case anyone tries to get rid of the device that launched the dart or darts," Helen explained.

"What should I be looking for? A long pipe would be easily spotted."

Rex shrugged, at a loss. "I imagine it could be any length."

"If we found it, we might be able to judge the distance from which the dart was shot," Alistair suggested. "Or else an expert could. That might help a great deal."

"Aye, it would, if we could remember who was standing where. Many of the guests' memories will be blurred by booze."

"Mine being no exception. Could I get some of that coffee?" Rex's colleague asked. "I'm beginning to feel a bit sluggish. I wish now I hadn't drunk so much whisky."

"You and me both. Aspirin?"

"Whatever's going," Alistair said gratefully, accepting a mug of coffee from Helen, who always seemed to remember how much cream and sugar everyone took. He palmed the aspirin Rex offered. "Thanks. Hopefully, this will prevent a hangover headache. Look, you don't suspect John, do you?" he asked standing awkwardly by the kitchen table.

"No particular reason to at this point," Rex hedged.

"Right. Because he could never do anything like this. For goodness sake, he's in the business of saving lives, not taking them."

This was not a convincing argument in Rex's book, since he had prosecuted several cases in his career where doctors, nurses, and hospital orderlies had finished off a patient for a variety of reasons. In many instances, it wasn't even personal. They had believed they were pursuing a sacred mission, or else had a God complex, or suffered from Munchausen by Proxy. A sad case, which Rex had tried with ambivalence, involved a medical practitioner who had performed euthanasia on a cancer-ridden patient in the last throes of agony. Rex rubbed his tired eyes to dispel the memory of the dignified and unrepentant doctor.

"Are you okay, sweetheart?" Helen asked, rubbing his shoulder blades.

"Aye, I was just having morbid thoughts. Look, Alistair, in the interest of diligence and impartiality, we need to suspect everyone equally for the time being."

"Even Julie?" Alistair demanded, clearly upset that John was not being removed from the suspects list.

"Even Julie," Rex said before Helen could comment. "Fair's fair. However, it's highly unlikely Julie is involved. She doesn't have any connection to these people, except Drew Harper. This is only her second visit to Scotland in recent years. Plus, her attention has been focused all night on Drew that I can see. On that point, I don't see how he could have made a move without her noticing."

"Unless they were in on the murders together... Look, would she even say anything is she saw Drew up to no good?" Alistair asked tellingly. It was clear he had noticed her infatuation with the house agent. "Aside from overreacting when he went over to chat with Zoe?"

"Alistair," Helen exclaimed in a chiding voice. "Please. If Julie saw Drew blow a dart into one or other of the Frasers, or both, I do believe she would have said something! She may be besotted but she's not a fool. I've known her for years and we're very close," she finished off firmly.

"I take your point, Helen. I'm just saying that suggesting John is capable of murder is as ludicrous as accusing your friend Julie."

"Nobody's suggesting anything of the sort," Rex placated his friend. "And you haven't known John as long as Helen has known Julie."

Alistair stood cradling his mug of coffee, staring into it. "Aye, but I know him in every sense. When you're that close to someone, you learn what they're capable of. And of murder, he isn't."

Well, they did say love was blind, Rex reflected. Was it worth reminding his legal colleague of family witnesses who had sworn on the bible that the defendant couldn't have committed whatever gruesome crime he or she was accused of, only for a guilty verdict to be returned? Probably not. "Be that as it may, let's assume, for the sake of thoroughness, that John and Julie are as potentially guilty as anyone else."

"Fine," Alistair said curtly.

Helen kept her mouth firmly shut.

"Now, one of us needs to be in there keeping watch. In fact, you both go and find out from Julie and John, respectively, if anyone left the room in our absence."

"What are you going to do, Rex?" Helen asked on her way out of the kitchen with a tray laden with cups, sugar, and cream, having refused his help. Alistair followed with the coffee pot.

"Make a call."

Rex dialled the number of Chief Inspector Dalgerry at Fort William Police Station and, eventually getting him on the line, after waiting for him to call back, explained the situation at

Gleneagle Lodge and expressed his concern that the police had not yet arrived.

The chief inspector assured him that assistance was on its way. "The dispatcher, who knows my son, called me at home, Mr. Graves. He thought I would like to know since it was your place, again."

Dalgerry had headed up the Moor Murders Case and, although Rex had solved the crime, he had let the chief inspector take most of the credit. Rex wasn't so much interested in fame as in the satisfaction of finding out *whodunit*. The two of them engaged in a cautious professional acquaintance, the officer according Rex grudging respect, and Rex, in turn, cognizant of the chief inspector's rank and experience.

"Aye, I'm beginning to regret buying this place. It was supposed to afford me some peace and quiet."

Dalgerry chuckled over the phone.

"Och, you love all the drama. And from what I hear, this one's a real gem. I'm in my car now heading up the A82, approximately half an hour away, depending on road conditions, which are verra bad." The chief inspector spoke in a growl, with a heavy Highland accent.

Rex thanked him and rang off while some charge was still left on his mobile phone. He sat quietly at the kitchen table to reflect on what could most expediently be achieved in the short time before the police arrived. Little progress had been made other than the discovery of the dart, which in and of itself was certainly important, except that it could have been shot by almost anyone in the room, and just conceivably by someone not invited to the party.

9
A HERO'S TALE

Without the other piece of the weapon, it was impossible to tell how far the dart had travelled in Ken's case. The roughly symmetrical wound suggested a direct shot. What level of expertise had been required to deal a fatal blow to Ken, and who possessed such expertise?

Unlikely it was Vanessa. The idea was almost laughable. Nobody truly believed it was her dart, even though it had been found in her clutch. She had offered a plausible reason for having it and had been believable; unless she was a consummate actress, and her daughter took after her in that department. Rex ran agitated fingers through his beard and flung himself back in his chair. Think, think, he exhorted himself, staring up at the ceiling. A pipe, or whatever device had launched the dart, must exist, else why would the killer have used a dart? And it was imperative they locate any remaining darts. Rex wished they had adequate light to make a thorough search and speed up progress. Presumably the police would come prepared. However, he wanted to find more evidence before anyone had a chance to hide anything.

He pushed himself out of the kitchen chair and went to re-join his guests, surprised to find them listening intently to Ace Weaver in his wheelchair. It appeared the old man was regaling them with a tale of escape from Flanders when his Spitfire was shot down in 1943 by a German Focke-Wulf 190 fighter. He now formed an integral part of the group, his wheelchair turned about, and he seemed remarkably revived. His voice, though it quavered in places, was strong, his eyes bright and alert. His wife nodded and expressed surprise at appropriate moments even though she must have heard his war stories numerous times before. Zoe regarded her father fondly and twiddled a long tendril of coppery hair.

Rex sat down beside Helen on the sofa and waited, all but writhing with impatience, until the ex-airman finished narrating his story of an adolescent boy in brown cap and loose trousers hiding him in an applecart in the meadow while the Germans searched the farmhouse and outbuildings, one of them going so far as to prod him under the fruit with a pitchfork, almost discovering him. In the nick of time, the quick-witted Emile, for that was the boy's name, created a diversion by drawing the soldiers' attention to the pilot's leather flight jacket floating in a marsh, compelling them to wade in and search while Ace made his escape on a bicycle disguised as a peasant, complete with beret and a string of onions hanging from the handlebars.

"I had a Gauloise dangling from my lips and a pair of spectacles with the lenses punched out," he recounted. "Emile even rubbed some flour in my eyebrows to make me look older. I was only twenty-one at the time—younger, I think, than anyone in this room. The Channel was heavily guarded by German patrols, and the Belgian Resistance took me to Paris where I hid for a week in a safe-house. A Basque guide led me and two American airmen through the Pyrenees into neutral Spain, and then to Gibraltar, a British colony."

Ace continued to address his audience. "It was a long way back home, but I was one of the lucky ones. Many didn't survive the crash landings or were shot while escaping, or else were sent to POW camps. If Vanessa and I had had a son, we would've called him Emile," he added wistfully. "Zoe finally came along, when we had all but given up hope."

He smiled at his daughter, and Rex caught a glimpse of the younger man. Ace must have been almost seventy when Zoe was born.

"Zoe's first name is Emilia," his wife told the group. "But she thinks it's too old-fashioned and uses her middle name."

Zoe rolled her eyes. "It's awful. Emilia Weaver. Not exactly a brilliant stage name."

Her mother sighed.

"That's quite a story, Ace," Drew said with admiration, leaning back on the loveseat.

"Yes," Helen agreed. "All it needs is a secret romance with a pretty Belgian girl."

Rex gave her a discreet nudge, as he wanted to move on, but it was too late. A look of sweet reminiscence lit

Ace's watery blue eyes.

"There was such a one," he began with a devilish smile. "Her name was Lisette." And then he gave an apologetic smile to his wife. "Vanessa was but a baby then."

"I wasn't even born!" she objected with a laugh, apparently forgetting, as had the others, the small matter of murder recently perpetrated in the house.

"Bravo to the brave airmen of the RAF," Alistair said.

Ace Weaver bowed his head in modest acknowledgment, but perhaps also in memory of lost comrades, Rex thought. *"Lest auld acquaintance be forgot"* would hold special meaning for him, no doubt.

"Thank you for sharing your war memories with us," Rex said. "But to return to less heroic feats, I can report that I have spoken to a Chief Inspector Dalgerry, and he will be with us shortly."

Sighs of relief and a few claps of applause followed Rex's announcement.

"What's taken the police so long?" Alistair asked, glancing at the mantelpiece clock.

"I understand the chief inspector decided to head up the investigation himself and has been busy putting a team in place."

"I remember Chief Inspector Dalgerry," Flora said. "He probably thinks the case is in safe hands until he gets here." She smiled with encouragement at Rex.

"Thank you, Flora. I can't say how sorry I am to subject you to a second investigation here at Gleneagle Lodge. You probably won't ever want to visit again."

"I feel quite safe with you," she said with heart-warming confidence. "I only hope you can solve this case as quickly as the last one."

"Well, I don't have much time. Still, it might help keep us awake if we used the rest of the wait time productively by continuing our search. What say you all?"

His suggestion met with a lukewarm reception. A sense of apathy from the strain appeared to be setting in, and no doubt most of the company would have been happy to let the police take care of the search, which would have to be done all over again, in any case.

"What will the chief inspector say if he hears we've been meddling with the investigation?" Professor Cleverly asked with a wry grin, rousing himself on the loveseat.

"Oh, he won't mind," Flora said. "Less work for him. He really didn't do much at all last time except charge about like a bull in a china shop."

Rex suppressed a chuckle. This was indeed a fair description of

Dalgerry's activity at Gleneagle Lodge that fateful summer. However, he didn't want to appear disrespectful. "Chief Inspector Dalgerry didn't get to his position because of his daintiness," he pointed out. "More from dogged perseverance and bullheadedness." He smiled in spite of himself. Dalgerry was indeed a bulldog.

"Now," he said, setting the coffee cups to one side of the table. "I expect we were all prepared to be up until the wee hours in any case, even if it wasn't for this unfortunate business."

"What a way to start a new year!" Drew lamented.

"Well, we can't turn back the clock," Julie said tartly, seemingly less enamoured of Drew. "Might as well get on with it and try to find out who did away with poor Ken and Catriona."

"I wish they could speak to us," John remarked, glancing over at the sheet-enshrouded bodies.

"It's possible they didn't even know what hit them," Vanessa said. "I hope not, anyway. Is whatever you said a fast-acting poison?" she asked Professor Cleverly.

"Curare paralyzes and asphyxiates the victim," he said, smoothing his head. "It won't have been very quick."

"Oh dear." Vanessa Weaver's features sagged in distress.

This time it was her daughter who consoled her, and not the other way around. "The killer is not among us." Zoe turned to Rex. "While you were in the kitchen, we discussed who was the most likely suspect and drew a blank. We decided the most logical culprit is long gone."

Rex decided it could do no good to alarm the innocent or alert the guilty to his suspicions. "I hope you are right, Zoe. Perhaps finding some more clues will point in that direction. First, whose bag have we not checked yet?" One such article remained on the table, untouched since the earlier search, the guests assured him when he enquired. Helen and Julie who were staying at the lodge had not brought their handbags downstairs.

"This black one is mine," said Señora Delacruz, sitting straight and poised on a loveseat beside the professor. She had not appeared to flag all night, whereas the others looked jaded and dishevelled for the most part, except Cleverly who had no hair to speak of to begin with.

"This will entail further invasion of privacy, I'm afraid," Rex apologized once more.

"Perhaps we should give the men a turn and see what comes up in the rest of their pockets?" Margarita Delacruz put a fresh cigarette in her black lacquer holder and held it to her lips, clasping the professor's hand as he lit the end with a lighter engraved with her initials.

"I've only found handkerchiefs, keys, wallets, phones, and breath mints so far," Alistair recapped.

"Handkerchiefs," Rex repeated, hit by a memory flash. "Whose was it that Catriona used? I recall someone offering her their hanky."

"It was mine," John said producing a bunched-up wad of white cotton from his pocket.

"When did she return it?"

"After Helen dressed her cut and she had no further need of it."

"The police might want to see that."

"It's a present from ma mum!" It could have been "mam" he said, referring to his mother. Either way, he sounded like a wee lad on the verge of tears.

"Poor little Jonny," Alistair teased his partner, who blushed and promptly surrendered the item to Rex. The white material revealed several large blood spots soaked through it.

Flora and Margarita looked away.

"I didn't find anything resembling a dart or anything that could propel one," Alistair concluded his inventory. "I haven't looked in the coat pockets yet, men's or ladies'. Shall I fetch them?"

Rex acquiesced with a nod. He had no objection to Margarita's suggestion. The order of the search did not matter. Alistair brought in the outdoors apparel from the hall, which he had not got to earlier. He and Cleverly had kept their jackets on, as had Rex, who pulled out his pocket linings to show he had nothing in them. He drew his pipe out of his corduroys and patted down his other pocket to make sure it was empty. Nobody seemed to expect any surprises from him, but out of common courtesy and consideration for his guests he felt he could not hold himself exempt from the search.

Alistair put on one of the latex gloves and began fishing in pockets. "This is John's," he said indicating the medic's dark blue anorak. He extracted what looked like a small television remote from one of the outer pockets.

"What is that?" Margarita enquired.

"A Breathalyzer." John explained he had purchased it at Boot's pharmacy chain. "Alistair won't get into the car of an evening when it's my turn to drive unless I test my alcohol level."

"A wise precaution." Margarita inclined her head in approval.

"How did you get stuck with being the designated driver for New Year's Eve?" Julie asked.

"I bribed him," Alistair said.

"We tossed a coin," John corrected.

His mittens were stuffed into another pocket, but that was all there was. Alistair continued to sift through the other coat pockets. None produced a dart or anything else of a menacing nature, except for a penknife found in Jason's fleece, along with, less noteworthy, his car keys and two old rugby tickets, some sweet wrappers, and a used tissue.

"Good time as any to get rid of this rubbish," Alistair said with evident distaste, being of a fastidious nature.

"Better not dispose of anything yet," Rex said, putting the Breathalyzer and penknife aside on the table.

One of Cleverly's pockets yielded a spectacle case and a brown leather bookmark with gold lettering, which the professor was delighted to be reunited with, remarking that he had looked for it everywhere. Drew's Burberry overcoat offered even less of interest: lip salve, a comb, and a small bottle of cologne. A disappointing find when all was said and done, Rex thought. And nothing in the women's coats either.

"The contents of men's pockets do reflect the personality of the owner, don't they?" Flora commented.

"Like props," Zoe agreed.

"Everybody seems in character so far. Jason's were predictably messy!" Flora playfully backhanded him on the arm.

"Thank goodness, no guns or lethal spray," Jason exclaimed, wiping his brow in jest.

Zoe giggled. "Or voodoo dolls with pins stuck in their eyes."

"Really, Zoe. No need to be ghoulish on an occasion like this." Vanessa handed over to Rex a canvas hold-all located by her husband's wheelchair. "Ace didn't bring a coat."

Mr. Weaver had come wrapped in his travelling blanket. His bag was packed with an extra sweater, a bottle of prescription medicine, a container of nonsteroidal anti-inflammatory drugs, a pair of reading glasses in a soft tubular case, and a change of underclothes. Rex went through the articles carefully without taking any out of the bag. Vanessa rewarded his delicacy with a nod and smile of gratitude. He and Alistair decided to refrain from searching the invalid's person.

"I need to go to the loo," Flora complained.

So, it transpired, did a couple of other guests. Rex assured them he would allocate sufficient lighting to the cloakroom just as soon as they were through with the search. A few others, who hadn't already done so, wanted to make phone calls letting people at home know they might be held up at the lodge. They were all growing weary. Rex asked for everyone's patience while he quickly proceeded with the last bag.

The tasselled accessory belonged to Margarita. It was covered in bluish black sequins and opened with an old-fashioned twin clasp. He removed a delicately embroidered handkerchief, a small pill box containing what the señora said were aspirin, and which resembled the aspirin in the kitchen, a tortoiseshell comb, scarlet lipstick in a gold-plated capsule, a sample tube of moisturizer, and a slim leather purse holding British and Venezuelan notes and several credit cards.

"Everything seems to be in order here," Rex said, preparing to give the bag back to the owner, when his fingers encountered a small bulge in a zipped pouch tucked inside. He opened it and found secreted in the silk lining a dart identical to the one Vanessa had allegedly picked up earlier that night. His throat went dry, his heartbeat quickened.

A second dart in a second bag? This, indeed, was progress.

Without a word, he went down the hall to his study and compared the dart to the original he had locked away in his desk. He returned to the living room and found the same shocked silence as when he had left, everyone rigid and casting furtive eyes about, no one yet daring to accuse the lady who sat calmly taking puffs of her cigarette, her head tilted in an attitude of remote contemplation. Rex waited for her to tell him she had found it somewhere, just as Vanessa had come by hers, though he felt less inclined to believe her if that was the case. It would be too much of a coincidence.

"Well, Margarita," he prompted. "Can you give us an explanation as to why this dart was found in your possession?"

"Is it not obvious?"

"Is it?" Out of politeness and caution, he felt reluctant to ask her outright if she had murdered the Frasers. The tension in the room was palpable. Seconds passed away, the steady tick-tock of the clock interrupted only by the percussion of a log cracking apart in the fireplace and the symphony of wind blowing outside.

"What is obvious?" Rex tried again.

"That someone put it there."

"Oh, I see." Evidently, he was not going to get a ready confession. "Are you saying someone framed you?"

"That is correct. You cannot possibly think I would be so foolish as to hide a poison dart in my bag if I were the killer."

"That pocket is well hidden. I almost missed it."

"The police would have found it."

"If it were not got rid of first. Perhaps you did not have the opportunity after Vanessa's dart was found and the bags were being watched."

"You believe Vanessa and not me?"

Rex scratched an ear. "Vanessa was able to supply a reasonable explanation as to why a dart was found in her bag. Not that your explanation is without merit," he hastened to add. "Someone could have planted it." He looked around the closed expressions of those present and got the impression they all found her guilty. And why not? She was the most enigmatic person among them, and was, after all, from a part of the world whence similar darts originated.

"I can't believe Margarita had anything to do with this," Cleverly protested somewhat belatedly, and more out of gallantry, Rex suspected, than conviction.

"Am I supposed to have murdered the poor man in the hall?" she demanded of Rex. "I was never in the hall. At least, not since I first arrived. I have been in the living room all night."

"You could have shot at him with a pipe," Jason said.

"Ridiculous."

"Do we know for sure when Ken left the room?" Alistair asked Rex. "He was here for 'Auld Lang Syne,' but I can't remember what everyone was doing during those moments when we were discussing who might be at the front door. Or after that, and before we started looking for him. Can anyone recall?"

Most everybody shook their head and redirected their attention to Margarita Delacruz. Was she strong enough to have dragged Ken's stocky build into the broom closet? Rex assessed her tall, lithe frame and decided it was improbable.

"I was by the fire," she protested. "I was trying to stay warm. Brrr," she said, hugging herself in her black cashmere shawl. "The weather in this country!"

"It was dark," John said. "Anyone could have been anywhere."

"Humphrey took a candle and went to answer the door," Rex said, replaying the sequence of events in his mind. "No sign of Ken then, or when I entered the hall shortly afterwards to fetch the oil lamp from the kitchen. I brought it to the living room and stoked up the fire. When I went back into the hall to check the fuse box, I ran into Jason returning from the cloakroom, and he said he hadn't seen Ken either. Beyond that, details are a bit vague. And, as John said, it was dark."

Vanessa Weaver leaned forward in her armchair. "Margarita, dressed as she is all in black, could have slipped out of the room unnoticed."

"I'm wearing black too," Helen said.

Margarita gave her a grateful look and turned one of scorn upon Vanessa.

"Excuse me," came Ace Weaver's quavering voice from the wheelchair. "The lady was near me after the dance. She asked me, 'Is that someone at the door so late?' I explained about our Scottish tradition of first-footing. 'It is strange,' she said. 'It felt just now as though someone walked over my grave.' She gave a violent shiver. I remember it vividly. I asked her if she was all right, and she said she would take a brandy and asked if I would like one too. She went over to the drinks cabinet and poured us each one. I recall her telling me she didn't like the taste of whisky. She brought me some shortbread too. We exchanged toasts. Our glasses are here on the table. Hers has the lipstick on it."

Rex picked up the glass and examined it. It did indeed match the shade of red on her mouth. And there were shortbread crumbs down the front of the old man's flannel shirt peeking beneath his sweater and cardigan. Rex was struck by the clarity with which Ace had recounted the scene. He glanced at Vanessa, who did not seem pleased with her husband, whereas Margarita looked triumphant at being vindicated.

"You are not to drink alcohol without my knowledge, dear," his wife reprimanded. "You are on medication."

"I have not taken my medication today. It makes me confused."

"You are incorrigible," his wife said, failing to cover her irritation.

"It's Hogmanay, after all, Mum," Zoe said in defence of her father.

Rex wondered how reliable Ace Weaver's memory was. He addressed a questioning look at Vanessa, which she apparently understood, since she proceeded to inform him that her husband did remember the most recent of events and those from his distant past. The main difficulty seemed to be in recollecting what happened in between, when it all became a bit hazy.

"It's true," Zoe confirmed. "Dad's mind is very sharp unless he's been asleep for a long time, like overnight. Then he's a bit disorientated first thing in the morning. I don't think he should be taking all those pills." She stroked her father's cheek, her hair glowing the colour of flame in the firelight.

An endearing scene, Rex acknowledged while reflecting that, if the recent memory of a ninety-odd-year-old man was to be trusted, and Margarita had not left his sight, she could not have poisoned Ken Fraser. That left Flora and Jason, Vanessa, Zoe, Alistair, and Drew unaccounted for. When the knocking had sounded at the front door, he had discussed with Helen, Julie, Humphrey, and possibly John, the question of who might be calling so late. Rex thought it was John's voice he had heard, but he couldn't be sure. It could have been Jason's.

"Who was it that said a tall dark stranger was good luck as opposed to a redhead?" he asked the gathering.

"That was me," John said. "It's common knowledge."

"Rubbish," said Cleverly.

Time was running out, and though he now had a second piece of evidence, he was only one step closer to identifying the killer—by eliminating Ace and Margarita from the list of suspects, at least for the murder of Ken Fraser.

"Why use a dart?" Drew enquired of no one in particular. "Why not just poison the chocolates, for instance? Lord knows, I almost choked on one of those things."

"Curare is not harmful if ingested," Professor Cleverly supplied. "And it has a very bitter taste."

"But what if it isn't what you say?"

"It may not be," the professor conceded.

"Have you had first-hand experience with this particular poison?" Alistair asked.

"Only second hand, through my research."

"If the Frasers were targeted specifically," Alistair said, "the killer had to be sure the poison got to the right people. Chocolates would be more hit-and-miss."

"And if the killer had poisoned the chocolates, he or she would have to be one of us, which I still refuse to believe," Zoe stated, folding her slim arms across her décolleté.

Rex could not see how the girl did not freeze in her diaphanous green gown. It made him chilly just to watch her. As though reading his thoughts, Vanessa again told her daughter to put on her cardigan unless she wanted to catch her death of cold. At this unfortunate choice of words, a few pairs of eyes slid toward the bodies of Ken and Catriona Fraser. Rex had not wanted to move them out of the room before the proper authorities examined them. They had only removed Ken from the closet, so John could look him over more thoroughly.

"Who brought the chocolates, anyway?" Drew asked.

"I did," Vanessa replied tartly. "And they haven't been tampered with, I assure you."

"They were greatly appreciated," Rex hurriedly put in, to unruffle her feathers.

However, no one seemed inclined to have any more of them.

"There's another bag here," Zoe announced, reaching behind the armchair occupied by her mother, and pulling a large leather pouch up by the strap. "I only just noticed it when I was looking for my cardigan."

"It must be Catriona's. I forgot she would have brought one." Rex had qualms about looking inside the dead woman's bag, but it was necessary to leave no stone unturned if he hoped to find her killer. However, he only found the usual contents, plus a plastic Lshaped inhaler.

"Catriona had asthma," Professor Cleverly explained. "She suffered an attack when we were walking up to the castle one time. Do you remember, Drew?"

Nobody said anything, no doubt feeling the pathos engendered by the deceased's now redundant inhaler.

"Did Ken have a coat?" Rex asked, trying to remember what Mr. Fraser was wearing when he arrived. The Weavers had pulled up just ahead, and his attention had been taken up by assisting Vanessa and John get the old man out of the station wagon and into the house.

"Perhaps he hung it up in the cloakroom instead of on the coat stand in the hall," Alistair suggested, getting up and moving in that direction with his light.

He returned with a heavy trench coat and began going through the pockets, turning out keys, a wallet, a twisted gas station receipt, a bar magnifier, a bottle of eye drops, and a half-eaten Cadbury bar in its wrapper. This concluded the search of personal items, which Rex had been inventorying in his notebook—unless something was concealed on a guest's person outside their pockets. And he wasn't going to presume so far. He would leave that to the police.

Nor did he wish to subject the darts to further handling. Perhaps he could experiment with a similar missile composed of one of his fly fishing lures of similar size and weight. He consulted the guests regarding potential dart launchers and soon a collection of items cluttered the coffee table, including Ace Weaver's rubber-ended walking stick. This had been Flora's suggestion, which no one took seriously, although it was certainly long enough and was apparently hollow. At this stage Rex didn't want to rule anything out.

The old man had propelled himself closer to the table to watch the proceedings. The empty plastic pen Jason had produced when they were getting ready to write down their resolutions consumed most of Rex's attention, as did Margarita's cigarette holder. Only, the señora had not killed Ken Fraser, if Ace Weaver's alibi was true. She continued to maintain a stoic silence in the face of being shunned by the other guests.

What other device would serve to dispatch a fatal dart? "Ken's pipe?" Rex wondered aloud.

"Won't work," John said. "I pulled it from his trouser pocket when I was examining him. Even if the bowl screws off, the stem's curved."

In any case, Ken would have kept it on his person, Rex reasoned, and therefore it was unlikely the killer improvised with it. Before he could make further headway with his experiment, he heard the wail of sirens through the wind gusts, and could not decide if he was disappointed or relieved.

10
CLAN BLOOD

Rex opened the front door. The sleet had stopped, the storm was winding down. He welcomed Chief Inspector Dalgerry into his home and excused the lack of lights. The detective, squat in build, did indeed put Rex in mind of a British bulldog: pug nose, jowls, and all. He wore a dark, ill-fitting waistcoat beneath an open overcoat, suggesting he had been celebrating Hogmanay in style.

"More murders then," he said without preamble. "Bit of a death magnet, your Gleneagle Lodge. Sure they are dead?"

Two blue and yellow-on-white squad cars with flashing roof lights delivered their passengers into the windy night.

"We have a medic on hand who's a guest. The ambulance never came. I suppose someone cancelled it when we realized the victims were dead."

"He checked pupils and pulse?" Dalgerry wiped his shoes on the mat and moved into the dark hall. Rex left the door ajar for the new arrivals.

"Of course."

"Where are the bodies?"

"In the living room." Rex pointed down the hall to the dimly lit doorway.

"Poison, you said on the phone. You sure?"

"We found what appear to be two poisoned darts. Two bodies. Ken and Catriona Fraser. Not sure how the darts were administered yet."

"Perhaps they were jabbed into the bodies direct?" Dalgerry suggested.

"Just seems an elaborate plan if you are going to be that close to a victim, to use a dart in the first place."

"Aye. Why not some run-of-the-mill rat poison in the whisky or tea?" The chief inspector sighed heavily.

"Aye, verra strange. Well, let's get on wi' it," he said as a wiry man in plain clothes reached the doorstep carrying a high-power torch. Dalgerry introduced him as Detective Sergeant Milner. He told him to take a look at the victims in the living room and to ask the guests to remain where they were until they could be interviewed.

Flora passed the detective sergeant in the hall. Looking over her shoulder, she gave the chief inspector a brief timid stare before disappearing into the cloakroom, where a candle had been deposited for the guests' benefit.

"By the way, Happy Hogmanay to you and yours," Dalgerry said. He appeared to bestow this blessing without any hint of irony, and Rex wished him likewise.

"We were entertaining at home," the chief inspector informed him. "Big bash. Ah, well."

After jotting down the sequence of

events leading up to the murders per Rex's recollection, he gave further instructions to Milner, who had come back and confirmed the lifeless status of the two victims. Meanwhile Flora emerged from the cloakroom and returned to the living room.

The uniformed constables spanned out from the front door in a search of the courtyard while Milner assigned one officer to examine the side window of the living room from outside. He sent another to the patio off the kitchen door, where Rex remembered seeing shoe prints. No one but the crime scene technicians and emergency personnel were to be allowed on the property. A constable equipped with a logbook was given the unenviable task of stationing himself at the end of the floodlit driveway to carry out this directive.

Detective Sergeant Milner seemed disgruntled to be on duty as he shouted out orders, sounding like a drill sergeant hurling insults at privates. "Watch where you put your feet, you dunderheaded clodhoppers!" rang out loud and clear from outside. Rex closed the front door as much to shut out his voice as the penetrating cold.

"So, no sooner was 'Auld Lang Syne' sung than murder came calling," Dalgerry said ponderously. "Aye, verra strange case, indeed." He asked to see the bodies, expressing his displeasure at Ken Fraser having been moved from his original position.

"I don't suppose he was killed in the broom cupboard," Rex contended, opening the door to the cramped space under the stairs. "I think the killer moved him in there to hide him."

The chief inspector looked inside and nodded. "We'll get this photographed and sketched in due course. How did you find him?"

"Drew Harper, a guest, was looking for him downstairs while I was searching outside with Alistair Frazer and John Dunbar, the medic. Drew told us he had found him. Ken Fraser was sitting against the back wall. At first we thought he had had passed out, not passed away."

"This Drew Harper, he didn't touch him or disturb anything?"

"Not to my knowledge. At least, not before he helped remove him. John went in to check Ken first."

"So, we shouldn't expect to find any other of the guests' fingerprints in there unless it's the killer's?"

Rex thought for a moment. Had John removed his mittens before looking Ken over in the closet? Probably, but he couldn't recall. "Only Drew's and John's," he confirmed.

"And the woman. She's the deceased's wife, right? What aboot her?"

"We heard her gasp and tumble back into an armchair. It was dark. We thought at the time she had tripped and then fallen asleep on the spot. Both guests had partaken of a fair amount of alcohol."

"You mean they were drunk?" Dalgerry asked as he followed Rex in the direction of the living room.

"Ken, possibly. Catriona Fraser was in good spirits and a wee bit clumsy." Rex felt obliged to protect the deceased woman's reputation as far as was truthful.

"Drunk," Dalgerry restated.

"Not quite," Rex qualified.

"But enough not to be in full control of their fate, either of them?"

"Aye, they would have been vulnerable at the hands of a vicious killer." Aside from possible impairment of reaction from alcohol, they were neither of them fit by the looks of it, and Catriona had been almost blind in her right eye, according to what her husband had said when she recounted her fall at the Glenspean Lodge hotel. He mentioned this detail to Dalgerry, who scribbled in his notepad, his torch tucked under his armpit, grouching all the while at the added difficulty of being without light.

"What do you know about the couple?"

"Well, not that much. I invited them because they were neighbours. That's their ancestral castle up on the hill."

Dalgerry looked sceptical. "You don't mean to say they had moved in there? It's a pile of old rubble. They'd have been more comfortable in your old stables!"

"I don't know if they intended to renovate the place, although they implied they might if they came into some money they hoped might become available."

"Money? Now we may be getting somewhere. 'Money, money, money,'" the chief inspector chanted. "Isn't that a song?"

"Something about it being a rich man's world? It was by the Swedish group ABBA. If that's the song you mean."

Dalgerry gave a rare chuckle. "ABBA. Och, aye. Takes me back. I met my missus at a disco. Her favourite song was 'Dancing Queen.' She could dance, my Kirsty." A warm glow of reminiscence infused the inspector's round brown eyes as he gazed at the wall.

Rex had difficulty envisioning the thickset chief inspector tripping the light fantastic, and wondered exactly how much whisky he had consumed for Hogmanay.

"Aye, well," Dalgerry collected himself. "Best take a look at the bodies and find oot what's what. Dr. Carmichael should be here shortly. She'll be doing the post-mortems. So

I'll only take a quick gander for now."

"What's she doing coming oot here?"

"Likes to see them before they land on the slab. Said it gives her a better perspective."

Rex wondered what she'd been doing on Hogmanay.

"Married to her job," Dalgerry said as though in answer to his thoughts. "I'll wait for her before I contact the PF." The procurator fiscal, a public prosecutor or coroner, investigated all sudden and suspicious deaths in Scotland.

They proceeded into the living room and he pulled back the sheet. In the semi-darkness Ken Fraser looked as though he were lying in somnolent repose on the sofa.

"Och, aye, that's a nasty deep puncture on his neck," Dalgerry said examining the wound, which Rex had exposed by pulling down on the grey-

and-white chequered scarf. "No other injuries?" he asked sweeping the body with the torch.

"None that I could see without removing more clothes."

"Well, we'll find oot soon enough. And the female victim. I don't see a mark on her neck." Dalgerry bent over Catriona Fraser, holding the flaps of his open coat pressed to his body with one hand. His jowls wobbled as he looked her over from head to foot.

"It's on her thumb." Rex peeled back the sticking plaster. "She cut herself on a piece of broken glass. I think the killer used this point of entry to facilitate absorption of the poison into the bloodstream, or else so he could hide it, as he did with the scarf on Ken."

"You say 'he,'" Dalgerry said straightening himself fully upright. "You suspect one of your male guests?"

"Not necessarily. These murders

could have been committed by a woman, I suppose."

"Do you have any ideas as to who might have done this?"

"I don't."

"So, the killer maybe knew aboot the cut on her thumb," Dalgerry said with an astuteness that possibly belied Rex's earlier impression that he had been at the whisky that night.

"So it would seem."

Dalgerry asked when the accident with the glass had occurred.

"Around nine."

"What poison did you say on the phone?" The chief inspector consulted his notes. "Not sure I got it down right."

"Curare."

"Sure aboot that? I've never heard of it."

"It's how Professor Cleverly identified it. He lectures in history at Edinburgh University, but he's an avid anthropologist. He said the compound, a brown sticky substance, is made out of poisonous bark found in the Amazon rainforest and used by the natives to kill their prey. It paralyses them and, though death can take up to half an hour in humans, the victim cannot use any of their muscles to alert anyone of their predicament. They cannot blink, point, or speak. They can only suffer in silence." Rex had questioned Humphrey further about the effects of curare in the final moments before the police arrived.

"Good God. What happens then?"

"They end up suffocating."

"Hm, verra interesting. But perhaps a wee bit far-fetched?"

Rex confessed that it was. "The totality of the circumstances is bizarre. A double poisoning of the last known survivors of a branch of the Fraser clan, heirs to an old castle reputed to be harbouring a cache of gold—"

Dalgerry shot him a look of surprise.

"I stress the word 'reputed.' It could all be nonsense, but the Frasers believed that part of the Loch Arkaig Treasure is buried there."

The chief inspector stamped his foot and turned around on the spot. "The Loch Arkaig Treasure belonging to Bonnie Prince Charlie? Och, man, ye canna be serious!" Incredulous stupor had rendered his Highland Scots all the more pronounced. "That's been lost for centuries. Why should it turn up now in your neck of the woods? I canna believe it! Any of it."

Rex toyed with the idea of revealing the existence of Jason's coin, but decided against it for the time being. He would prefer that the lad tell the police himself. It had been his find, after all. Of course, without Drew Harper's intervention, none of them would have been any the wiser. If

Jason had kept quiet about it since the autumn and not told his girlfriend, chances were he never would have confessed.

"What can you tell me aboot these people before I go over?" Dalgerry spoke in a low voice, glancing across at the weary group by the fireplace. "How well do you know them?"

"You'll remember my fiancée Helen from the Moors Murders Case. And Flora Allerdice."

"Aye, I thought I recognized the lass when she passed in the hall." She now sat with her back to them. "Brother Donnie, right? A bit slow."

"A good lad."

"How's your son Campbell doing?"

Rex was greatly impressed he remembered his son's name. "He's in Florida."

"Never followed in your footsteps, did he?"

"No, his passion is marine science."

"Ah, well, neither of my lads joined the police force. As you were saying..."

"Ehm, Helen's friend from Derby, Julie Brownley, is staying with us for a few days. She teaches at the school where Helen works. They've known each other for years. Drew Harper, the man sitting beside her, is a local house agent. He helped me look for a place in the Highlands. Alistair Frazer is another face you'll recognize from my summer housewarming party."

"A colleague of yours. I mind him clearly." Dalgerry made notes in his pad. "Any more from your previous party? Not planning on having any more, are you?" he asked, a bushy grey eyebrow raised in a circumflex.

"Not for the time being. Helen and I plan to hold our wedding in Edinburgh."

"Probably a good idea."

"John Dunbar was a medic in the previous case," Rex continued with the list. "That's how he and Alistair met."

Dalgerry stared across the room, where the two men sat together. "So, a total of four, besides yourself, who were here that other time. Right. Go on."

"The lad next to Flora is her boyfriend, Jason Short, also a student of art at Inverness College. Let's see. Vanessa Weaver in the purple dress was my interior designer for this place. She brought her husband and daughter. Ace Weaver is the gentleman in the wheelchair."

"Is he ambulatory?"

"Aye, but only with difficulty."

Dalgerry continued to make notes with his short yellow pencil on which the eraser was worn flat as a nail head.

"That leaves Margarita Delacruz, the professor's guest," Rex said.

"She must be the foreign-looking lady. Spanish?"

"From Venezuela, I believe. I found

currency from that country in her evening bag."

"Searched them all, did you?"

"That's how we found the darts. They were in the ladies' bags, hers and Vanessa's."

"What is the professor's full name?"

"Humphrey Lawrence Cleverly."

"And how well do you know him?"

"We were at university together, and then lost touch for many years. We ran into each other recently at a town and gown function in Edinburgh."

"And can you vouch for all these people?"

Rex hesitated before he said cautiously, "Tonight is the first time I've met Señora Delacruz, Jason Short, and Zoe and Ace Weaver. The rest have been to the lodge before."

The chief inspector reviewed his hieroglyphics. "Jason Short, that's Flora's boyfriend. And Vanessa

Weaver's daughter and husband. Got it. What does the daughter do?"

"She's an actress, or hoping to be."

"Looks the part, from what I can see. Wish we had more light. You called the power company, I assume?"

"Of course."

"I noticed other lights were oot around here."

"That's good. Hopefully those residents will have called as well."

"A fallen tree branch somewhere, I expect. What can you tell me aboot the old man? Looks harmless enough from where I'm standing."

"He was a fighter pilot in the Second World War. Ace is his nickname. Don't know what his civilian job was. Quite a sharp cookie for his age." Rex told the chief inspector about Weaver supplying an alibi for Margarita Delacruz at around the time Ken Fraser disappeared. "By the time I brought the oil lamp from the kitchen, everyone except Ken was present in the living room, and Jason whom I bumped into when I went back into the hall to check the fuses."

Dalgerry made a note. "We need to find oot more on the Frasers. The state of their finances, where they lived, any potential enemies, and so on. What did they do for a living, do you know?"

"I think I heard something aboot Ken being involved in an export business, supplying Scottish merchandise to the States. A huge market over there, I understand. Not sure aboot Catriona. They were both interested in genealogy. Theirs in particular. They were an offshoot of Clan Fraser, their ancestors having fallen oot of favour with the illustrious clan in the fifteen-hundreds. Seems a member of their immediate clan, Red Dougal, brought his small band of supporters to Gleneagle and built that castle."

"There could be a long-standing feud involved, then." Dalgerry wrote furiously on his pad. "Someone in the family could have wished them dead."

"I was led to believe they were the sole survivors."

"Och, just wait and see who crawls oot of the woodwork once news of their death gets oot. I don't suppose you know if they left a will?"

"I do not. I only know the castle could only be left to a clan member, and that person had to be married to someone in that branch of the clan."

"Sounds verra restrictive."

"It was meant to be, I suppose to make sure the castle stayed within the sub-clan."

"They had no children?"

"No. I don't think they've been married that long."

"So, no legally adopted heirs we could look at?"

Rex shook his head. "Not to my

knowledge."

"Pity. Still, the export business might be worth looking into. Partners and such, whether Ken Fraser had stiffed anyone, or else some mafia aspect."

Rex thought this last lead highly improbable, but the Russians were infiltrating everywhere nowadays. Perhaps they were diversifying into kilts, bag pipes, and sporrans. He held back a chuckle. Sergeant Milner approached them, removing his damp woollen gloves.

"Nothing of much interest so far," he reported. "I'm having the men follow the deer trail through the trees leading to the road."

"And what aboot around the window?" The chief inspector pointed behind him.

"Nothing appears to be disturbed on the ground. I'll have the examiners dust the window inside and oot, but chances are the killer wore gloves anyway on a night like this. Someone closed it, unfortunately."

"Aye, I can see that." Dalgerry turned to Rex for an explanation.

"Helen did, while we, that is, Alistair, John, Drew and I, were looking for Ken Fraser. With the central heating oot, it was beginning to get cold. And we didn't know anyone had been murdered at that point. We simply thought Ken had gone to get something from his car or else wandered off to a different part of the house."

"The exterior door to the kitchen was unlocked, you said, so an intruder could have come in that way. It's a moonless night and not much traffic on the roads around midnight on Hogmanay. Housebreakers often case remote properties over holidays to see if there's an opportunity to break in while the owners are away. You said you'd seen shoe prints ootside the kitchen door."

"While I was getting wood from the shed. They were visible in the slush on the doorstep and patio."

"We found quite a lot of foot traffic in that area," the detective sergeant said. "But only two different sets of prints on the patio. One shoe and one boot."

"I don't think those will be mine," Rex said. "I stuck to the path on the way to the woodshed. But one set could belong to John. He was searching for Ken at the back of the house and by the loch. And he's wearing boots."

"Right," Dalgerry told Milner. "One set of boot prints to confirm and one set of shoe prints to identify."

During the ensuing exchange between the police officers, Rex looked about him. The two white body sheets rose eerily out of the dimly lit room. The fire had died down, but enough candlelight filtered through the darkness to illuminate the pale ovals of the guests' faces as they slouched bundled up in their seats around the coffee table.

Rex tried to remember who had been standing where at the end of "Auld Lang Syne" when the lights went out. Helen had been beside him for the dance, Julie on his other side, Catriona and Ken opposite, Flora and Jason somewhere to his left. Beyond that, he couldn't be sure. The circle had broken up and people had moved about in the dark. Catriona had tripped or been pushed back into an armchair. Ken must have wandered off before then or he would have gone to his wife's aid.

Everybody would have to be questioned regarding their movements around midnight: A tedious prospect, but better to do so while events were still relatively fresh in the guests' memories, and before they could be influenced by other information. Milner, armed with his torch, went to take the guests' statements. The detective was just crossing the room when, all of a sudden, the lights came back on.

The miracle of artificial light! Rex could not have been happier if he had been the first cave dweller to discover fire. His was not the only euphoric reaction. Everyone blinked in the electricity and exclaimed with delight, relieved to have their basic comforts restored. Rex offered up a silent prayer of thanks. He switched on more table lamps. The living room suddenly looked smaller and more welcoming.

"Certainly makes our task easier!" Dalgerry said, rubbing his hands together. "Any chance of a cup of tea for me and the lads, if it's not too much trouble? And I seem to remember your lovely fiancée made excellent biscuits."

Was this the chief inspector's way of dismissing him, or had Helen's baking made that much of an impression? Still, Rex did not begrudge the police a cup of tea to warm them up. He cocked his head at Helen, and she rose from the sofa and came towards him.

"The chief inspector has requested tea for his team. I wondered if you'd like to keep me company in the kitchen while I make it, and he and DS Milner talk to our guests."

As they repaired to the kitchen and started the tea, Rex filled her in on what Dalgerry had imparted, none of which had been very helpful. He left out the mafia angle, and limited the chief inspector's hypotheses to a family feud or business dealings gone sour.

"So who *has* got a good motive for murdering the Frasers?" Helen asked.

"Me."

"You? Be serious, Rex."

"I am. The prospect of this serene spot being overrun by eager reporters and treasure hunters was raising my blood pressure."

"If the murders were premeditated, who knew about the gold?"

Rex thought for a moment. "Drew Harper, presumably. He was the house agent advising them. He saw Jason poking around the castle. And Catriona, who was a very open and trusting person, would have confided their interest in Gleneagle Castle, over and above the fact they were the heirs and wanted to keep it in the family. Humphrey knew, of course, and may have told Margarita, although she professed to know nothing aboot the gold. Jason, obviously, because he found the coin. He might have thought there'd be more. He might have gone back. That's a big lure, especially for an impoverished student."

"According to what Drew said, he wouldn't be able to sell his old coin or any others he found."

"There's always a black market for valuables. Paintings worth millions are stolen from galleries and museums and sold to private collectors."

Rex removed the hissing kettle from the vintage range, while Helen fetched down the tin of homemade biscuits from the pantry shelf. "Who will inherit the castle now?" she asked.

"I suppose in the normal way of things any family member found to be alive. I'm not entirely sure how that arcane old deed was structured. But didn't they say they were the last surviving heirs bar an aunt who disappeared?"

"Who knew the Frasers were going to be here?"

Rex smiled to himself. Helen was asking the questions, clearly intent on cracking the case. Just as well she went along with his morbid hobby, he thought. In fact, on their vacation in Key West, she had proved herself a worthy partner in a most bizarre case involving the owners of a guesthouse.

"Pretty much everybody present knew they'd be here," he replied. "I would have mentioned who was coming when I invited people. 'Oh, so-and-so's coming. You know them, don't you?' Or, 'You might be interested in meeting so-and-so.'"

"Maybe someone wanted to kill them for a reason other than the gold." Helen warmed the large earthenware tea pot and added an ample supply of loose Assam.

"What reason?" Rex enquired. He could not imagine Ken being ruthless in business or resisting the mafia. "They seemed like a very nice, ordinary couple. Ken was a bit of a bore, but boring someone to death is not a motive I've ever come across or heard applied literally."

"Flora doesn't like them. *Didn't*, I should say."

"No?" Rex reflected for a moment. "She barely spoke two words to them."

"Precisely. And didn't you say you first met the Frasers at the Loch Lochy Hotel?"

"Perhaps you're right. Flora was there. I should talk to her and perhaps call Shona for more information. But Flora's parents don't know she's here. They might be offended not to have been invited. I suppose there'll be no concealing it now. Funny, I never noticed Flora's attitude. But she and Jason have pretty much kept themselves to themselves all evening."

Helen gave a discouraged sigh. "We're not getting very far."

"Perhaps we're not meant to. We may be dealing with a truly cunning murderer."

"It couldn't be anything other than murder, I suppose?"

"Two well-directed poison darts? I doubt it was an accident and even less that they were self-inflicted. There are easier and less dramatic ways to kill oneself. In any case, the Frasers seemed happy and excited aboot their future."

"Could someone have killed them in a jealous rage? They married quite late in life. Perhaps a spurned ex was out for revenge."

"Hard to imagine either of them inspiring fits of passion."

"Now, now, Rex. We don't know what they were like when they were younger. But if they had no enemies," Helen concluded, "it must be the treasure someone was after. There were gold bars as well, apparently."

With no other leads, Rex made a note to ask Flora about her attitude toward the Frasers. She was a sensitive and secretive sort of lass, and still waters ran deep.

"We'll have to give the police the mugs," Helen said, looking in the cabinets. "We're out of cups."

"We can run the dishwasher now." Rex loaded the coffee cups from earlier.

Carrying the tea tray, he returned to the living room where the chief inspector and sergeant were busy interviewing the guests. He distributed the mugs of tea to the police taking a break in the hall, while Helen offered her oatmeal and raisin cookies. The crunch of vehicles on gravel brought them both to the door. Two vans and a sedan pulled up next to the squad cars. Scene-of-crime officers clad in white and equipped with cases descended first, followed by a middle-aged woman in a parker and sensible shoes carrying a doctor's bag, and, finally, a couple of male personnel with folded black body bags.

These made the recent events seem all the more real and disturbing. Ken and Catriona Fraser could not have deserved to die, whatever the motive.

11
THE MOURNFUL MORN

The guests relocated to the library while investigators took photographs and video footage of areas of particular interest. By four o' clock in the morning, the statements of everyone present at the party, including Rex's, had been gone over and validated by the chief inspector.

Under haughty protest, Margarita Delacruz had been questioned the longest due to the incriminating and inadequately explained dart in her handbag.

All but three of the Queen Anne style dining chairs had been brought into the library to supplement the padded leather desk chair, two wing armchairs, and an Edwardian daybed, on which Ace Weaver was installed and covered with his traveling blanket. He should have asked Ace, while the old man was still lucid, if he had noticed anything suspicious during the course of the night, but the police had arrived and taken over.

Rex had implored the Weavers to spend the night at the lodge, or what remained of it, even if the police released the guests sooner. He lit the electric fire in the grate. The library felt substantial and timeless, an effect created by the stained wood-paneled walls, shelves stuffed with excess books from his mother's Victorian house in Morningside, watercolors of local flora and fauna, parchment lamp shades, and an antique swivel globe atop a tripod table. He loved to work and read in here cocooned from the world.

"I wonder if the investigators have made any progress," Flora said after a while. "They've been at it for ages."

"They're certainly going over everything with a fine-tooth comb," Drew agreed through clenched teeth.

"Shouldn't be too long now," Rex said, though he couldn't really be sure. Dalgerry was nothing if not thorough.

Julie yawned and covered her mouth, stretching her stiletto-booted legs from her chair.

The simulated logs gave off a cheerful glow and radiant warmth, making everyone sleepier still. Professor Cleverly nodded off in a wing chair, while Ace Weaver slept soundly, his face half swallowed by a pillow. His wife, curled on a cushion at his feet, propped her head up on one hand, her elbow resting on the daybed, which had been recovered in russet velvet to match the drapes and faded oriental rug on the hardwood floor.

"I would so love to be in my bed," Zoe lamented. "Can't you do something, Mum?"

"Zoe. The detectives were very apologetic, especially in view of your father's condition, but they can't dismiss us until they're satisfied there's nothing more we can help them with."

"They're just waiting for one of us to crack and confess."

"Don't be ridiculous, Zoe. That only happens on TV."

Nerves and tempers were beginning to fray. Rex installed himself behind his antique desk with a compartmentalized box of trout flies before him. He never tired of looking at the delicate feathery creations—red, yellow, and patterned—fashioned around hooks, and which he purchased from a master fly fisherman in Gleneagle Village. He enjoyed standing on the loch shore or drifting out in his row boat, on rare occasions landing a wild brown trout, its back speckled silver. The flies were about the size of the poison darts. He lifted one out. It was, however, somewhat lighter.

"They must have searched everywhere by now," John complained as the clock on the shelf ticked away the minutes. "And they frisked everybody." A female constable had been brought in the lodge for the women. "So it's not as though any of us could have stuffed anything down our clothes. I really don't see the point in keeping us any longer."

Alistair was beginning to answer when he suddenly turned his head towards the door, where steps and voices could be heard approaching in the hall. Those guests drifting off sat up with a jolt when the chief inspector burst into the room with the detective sergeant on his heels. Rex wondered whether there had been a break in the case or if the guests were going to be told they were free to leave at last.

Dalgerry stopped in the middle of the room and spun on Drew. "Mr. Harper, your shoes, please."

Everyone stared at the house agent.

"You already took an impression of my shoes."

"Two sets of prints were found on the patio by the kitchen door. One set belongs to John Dunbar. We believe the others to be your dress shoes, but there are many overlapping prints, and we want to verify they're a match by superimposing them direct."

"The prints *are* mine," Drew expostulated, growing red in the face, but untying his laces nonetheless.

"And what were you doing ootside?"

"Making a call."

"Rather cold to be on the phone..."

"Overseas call. I wanted to be sure I could get a signal in this remote area."

"Why not from the front door?"

"Like I said, it was long-distance. I couldn't hear properly with people still arriving at the house."

"So you tried calling ootside the

front door first?"

"I... no. I just knew it would be difficult to hear. Have you ever made a long-distance call on a mobile phone in the middle of nowhere?" Drew demanded.

"Business?"

"Personal."

"Care to explain the nature of your call?"

"Not really." Drew, clutching his shoes, looked ready to chuck them at the chief inspector.

Milner went to retrieve them in a transparent bag and disappeared from the room.

"Perhaps at the station, then," Dalgerry said ominously.

"It was your girlfriend in America, wasn't it?" Julie accused Drew. "Why don't you just come out and say it? That's why you skulked out the back door."

Drew had the decency to look

abashed. He had been no less blunt when attacking Jason over the coin, Rex recalled. "Fine then. My call was to a Dr. Heather McCall in Chicago," he told the chief inspector. "I made the call around eight to wish her a happy new year before the party got under way. We only spoke for a few minutes."

Julie stared proverbial daggers at him.

"Correct," Dalgerry said referring to the handwritten phone records in his hand, having confiscated all the mobiles.

Rex moved around to the front of his desk and, clearing some objects out of the way, sat on its polished mahogany surface.

"Two minutes and fifty-eight seconds, to be exact," Dalgerry informed Drew, clearly ignorant of his relationship with Julie. "There are a lot of prints for such a short call."

"It's expensive calling the States

and it was cold, like you said. I pace when I talk on the phone. Especially in freezing temperatures."

"Shortly before midnight is when I went to the woodshed and noticed the shoe prints," Rex stated, deflecting attention away from his guest in his discomposure. "John's would have been added afterwards when he went to search for Ken Fraser."

"Right," the chief inspector addressed Rex. "If we can account for all the prints, we can exclude the theory that a stranger came in by that way. However," he said, dragging out the word for effect, "we did find tyre tracks by the side of the road at the top of your driveway. And muddy foot prints. Someone stopped there during the night. The prints are still fresh."

Everyone sat forward in their chairs except Ace Weaver, warmly tucked up on the daybed. This new evidence pointed to an intruder, a less threatening theory the guests would no doubt prefer to entertain. Rex could almost hear the relieved breath of eleven people being exhaled into the room, and none more relieved than the killer's, he thought, personally of the opinion that the murderer was still among them.

"A broken-down motorist?" he suggested.

"Any tracks leading down the driveway other than our cars' and those belonging to you lot?" John asked the chief inspector.

"We are trying to ascertain that at present."

Rex surmised the police would not be able to ascertain much in a hurry. Too many vehicles had churned up his driveway that night.

"It's possible someone spotted the suspicious vehicle in passing," Dalgerry went on, his use of the adjective "suspicious" alerting Rex to the fact that he adhered to the intruder theory. "And hopefully that witness will come forward once we make an appeal to the public."

Rex hoped Dalgerry wasn't going to go off at a tangent, as he had been known to do in the past. Hopefully, too, he had more concrete evidence.

"There is another item of interest." The chief inspector paused while he looked around the room to make sure he had everyone's attention. His gaze alighted on the daybed where Ace Weaver's sleeping form alone ignored his presence. His bulging eyes lingered on Vanessa seated at the invalid's feet. He then began walking about the room assessing each of the guests in turn. He stopped in front of Señora Delacruz and proffered a menacing smile. She recoiled in her chair and turned to Professor Cleverly with a look of entreaty. Humphrey sat up straighter, but said nothing.

"When am I going to get my shoes back?" Drew asked, arms crossed in defiance, his narrow feet clad in dark blue diamond-patterned socks.

"That depends, Mr. Harper."

Drew was about to say something, but apparently thought better of it. He simply glared at the chief inspector's back with undisguised contempt.

"A piece of clothing was found snagged on a tree." Dalgerry whirled back to face Rex. "Behind your house."

"Well, then. That underscores the theory of an intruder, doesn't it?" Julie asked.

"Especially if no one here is missing part of their clothing." Dalgerry glanced around the room and received puzzled shakes of the head.

He would already know the answer to that since everyone's clothes had been patted down and looked over. Rex was growing antsy. The killer would have had hours in which to compose himself or herself by now, and to think and plan.

"What sort of clothing?" John asked, as a paramedic no doubt used to dealing with the police and not afraid to ask questions.

"I'm afraid I cannot divulge that at present."

A torn piece of material had any number of explanations for being in the woods, Rex reasoned. It could have been blown there or else left by an innocent hiker; or not so innocent, since that person would have had to be trespassing on his land, but that was a negligible crime compared with two murders. Or it could have been deposited by Helen or Julie. However, in that case, he would have heard about some ruined clothing. He really couldn't tell much without seeing the item.

"How high up in the tree?" he asked.

Dalgerry bared jagged teeth at him in another simulation of a smile. "Perhaps you'd like to step into the hall with me."

Rex did so gladly, eager to find out what the chief inspector had to tell him in private.

Dalgerry led Rex to the kitchen, where the door leading outside had been sealed off with barricade tape. They sat down opposite each other in the breakfast nook.

"I won't detain your guests much longer," Dalgerry said. "None of their statements provided much of interest. Most were just a muddle with a common theme of events: the buffet, the buried gold, the parlor game, the dancing, the power cut, Catriona Fraser falling back into an armchair, the knock at the door after midnight, the search party. But not necessarily in that order, which is mainly based on your statement and that of your fiancée, and of Alistair Frazer and his friend, John Dunbar."

Once again, Rex was impressed by Dalgerry's powers of recall.

The chief inspector stretched out his stubby arms. "The bodies have been removed and the crime technicians are almost finished."

"What was the medical opinion as to cause of death?"

"Fatal paralysis caused by a drug or poison. Dr. Carmichael will know more after performing the autopsies. I told her you thought it might be curare in the entry wounds. She said she'd never had a case like this."

"I hope we know more soon."

"I wanted to show you this." Dalgerry opened a tablet computer that had been sitting on the pine table. He tapped on the screen and turned it around to face Rex. A bird's-eye view of his property showed the snow-dusted roof of the house, those of the stables and shed, dense areas of treetop, a snaking expanse of gray loch, and contours of hilly terrain.

"The piece of clothing was found here," Dalgerry said, rising out of his chair and leaning around the wireless device to point with a podgy finger at a spot on the map.

"I've used that trail myself. It leads over the glen to Loch Lochy, a five-mile walk. But it's a bit of a detour from the main entrance to Gleneagle Lodge."

"Aye. If the motorist came by that way, he would have had to walk up the road half a mile. If he was simply looking for assistance, he would have come down the driveway. You said the lights went oot just after midnight?"

Rex nodded. "Doubtful a motorist who'd broken down would have bothered to walk down the driveway if he thought the lodge was vacant. If he made it to the door and that was the knocking we heard, he decided not to stick around for long."

"What I'm thinking, Mr. Graves, is that this was no innocent motorist. We think the tyre marks belong to a van, judging by the distance between the wheels. And we got a good impression of the tread. An innocent motorist would have knocked and waited, lights or no lights, having made it that far on foot."

"Perhaps it was a housebreaker who thought the lodge was empty. And then, walking around the lodge, saw there were candles and a bunch of people inside. I'd drawn the curtains closed on the bay windows, but not on the side window because I was trying to air the room. The would-be intruder would have revised his plan to break in and rob me."

"Let's drop the hypothesis of a housebreaker for now and assume it was a person or persons of more sinister intent, who parked their van and came down by the trail, careful to cover their tracks, but leaving a piece of clothing on a spiky branch. They find the side window open and the house in near darkness and climb in unseen while the guests are preoccupied with the knock at the door, which was simply a diversion created by one of the miscreants."

"Did they wear night-vision goggles when they took aim at poor Ken?" Rex asked facetiously. "And if they went to the trouble of walking down the trail to avoid detection, why park their van at the top of the hill where any passing vehicle could see it?"

"You'd be surprised how daft some of these criminals are. That's usually how we manage to catch 'em."

"I don't think our killer is daft, somehow," Rex contended. "How many criminals have you come across who are familiar with curare and can shoot a dart with deadly accuracy?"

"Could be one of them tribesmen you mentioned," Dalgerry suggested. "All sorts are flooding into the United Kingdom since we opened our borders."

"Did the piece of clothing you found suggest a person from the Amazonian rainforests?" Rex asked with stark sarcasm. "They must find our climate a wee bit cold for their tastes."

"We found tufts of purple and white wool, but not enough to distinguish a pattern."

"Not the most clandestine of colours," Rex remarked. However, this information gave him pause. The colors for Inverness College were purple and white, he recalled from the brochure Flora had sent him with her joyful letter informing him of her admission to study art. "I see," he confined himself to saying. "I don't remember any of my guests wearing a garment in those colours."

"I suspect it was from a scarf or a bonnet, judging from the height you asked aboot." Dalgerry gave him a knowing wink. "And home knit, by the looks of it, not manufactured."

"It could have been the trailing end of a scarf, so it doesn't give an accurate height of the individual, does it? Unless it was from a bonnet."

"No," the chief inspector agreed. "Also, it was a wee bit grubby. No telling yet how long it was there or if it simply had not been washed in a while."

"Any footprints nearby?"

Dalgerry blew out a sigh. "Unfortunately not. Our perp covered his tracks, like I said."

"Or else the 'evidence' pre-dates the murders sufficiently for time to have erased any tell-tale signs. Or the wool blew into the tree in the gale."

The chief inspector shook his head vehemently. "It was well snagged on an overhanging branch. It caught, it was not blown there."

Rex was less convinced. The winds had been strong of late. "I have not taken that walk since, let me think...must be late summer. Any other evidence?" Rex asked, trying to contain his impatience. Tyre tracks on the road and a torn piece of knitted clothing two hundred feet from his house were not a lot to go on. "Anything inside the house?"

"Too many people and prints. It may take a while for the lab to get back to us with anything useful. But I did mean to ask you... Did you burn anything other than wood in your living room fireplace?"

"Just some newspaper earlier in the evening to get the fire going. Why?"

"We found a charred scroll of paper buried in the ash. Again, the lab will be able to tell us more."

"Ah," Rex said, remembering. "We were playing a game by the fire, writing down our New Year resolutions. Perhaps someone wrote something and then changed their mind, and later threw the paper in the fire."

"We found the jar containing the resolutions on the shelf above your drinks cabinet. Did everyone participate?"

"Aye, myself included. Vanessa Weaver wrote her husband's for him, as I recall. There should be fifteen names and one small piece of notepaper left over on the table, unless it was disposed of."

"There are fifteen notes in the jar, and one piece of paper missing, then. As you say, someone might have thrown their first try into the fire. But it might not be notepaper we found. The burnt fragment was stuck to some shiny red streamers."

Rex scratched at his beard. "I

wonder why someone threw a decoration in the fire?"

"Too much booze, I shouldn't wonder."

"What calls other than Drew Harper's to the States were made?" Rex asked viewing the upside-down phone records Dalgerry had deposited on the table.

The chief inspector referred to the sheet again. "Flora Allerdice called home on her phone in the wee hours after the murders were discovered. John Dunbar also called home. He said he still lived with his parents most of the time. That's all the calls since eight, when you said the guests started arriving. So it doesn't look as though someone called a hit man to give him the all-clear. Any calls made on your phone line before the power failed?"

"Not to my knowledge. At least, not during the time you're interested in." In the afternoon, Rex had called his mother in Edinburgh from his land-line to wish her happy new year. She didn't like to travel more than an hour in a car at a time, and had only visited the lodge on one occasion, when Rex had punctuated the trip with lunch. Helen had called her sisters early in the evening from her mobile phone, and Julie her divorced dad from hers.

"Do you mind if I ask my guests a few questions before you dismiss them? I'd like to address the paper in the fireplace."

"Fine, but don't mention the nature of the clothing we found. Neither the colour nor the fact it was wool."

"I won't, if it's information you wish to save for later," Rex assured him. He would find his own way around that obstacle.

"Let me know if you come up with anything. I need to check on the lads, and DS Milner is looking into a few things that might be of interest."

Dalgerry looked smug, and said no more.

Rex made towards the library to see what he could find out from the guests. Just as he was reaching for the door handle, the chief inspector called him back and asked him to wait a few moments while Milner, who had reappeared, reported his findings.

"Well, I'll be...," Dalgerry uttered after a brief conference with the detective. He pivoted towards Rex with a jubilant expression. "Mr. Graves," he said, "it appears you have an imposter under your roof."

12
A DARK HORSE

Dalgerry told Rex he would make the announcement in front of the guests. During questioning, none had professed to know of any aliases used by any of their fellow guests. Nor, said Dalgerry, did they admit to knowing anything that could conclusively lead them to believe anyone had a motive for killing the Frasers.

Rex took his place on the edge of his desk and waited for the chief inspector to make his revelation, though there was only one logical answer in his own mind as to the identity of the imposter.

"Won't keep you much longer," the officer informed the exhausted guests seated around the library. "And I have some news that may wake you up."

Murmurs of interest arose from the occupied chairs. Vanessa Weaver rubbed her eyes as though she had been asleep. Her husband's rhythmic raucous breathing was audible from where Rex sat gauging the guests' reactions. Helen stretched and yawned, and glanced with raised eyebrows at Rex, who shrugged. He would see if his supposition was correct.

A heavy-lidded Drew roused Julie. Zoe whispered something to John behind a cupped hand. Alistair, disengaged from the case since the police arrived, tilted his chair back on its hind legs and rocked to and fro, arms dangling by his side. They stared expectantly at Dalgerry, all of them pale and punch drunk from lack of sleep. Detective Sergeant Milner returned Drew's shoes with polite thanks and positioned himself at the library door, a human barricade, while Dalgerry spoke.

"It appears we have among us a person who came posing as a stranger to the Frasers for reasons that will no doubt be made clear in due course."

Señora Delacruz rose steadily from her chair in her black garb and amber beads, and said, "No doubt you are referring to me."

"Let me introduce Maighread Rose Fraser," Dalgerry announced with a grandiose gesture. "New claimant to Gleneagle Castle."

Rex had suspected as much, and no one else showed undue surprise. She was the likeliest imposter. But why had she kept her identity secret? There was on obvious reason.

"The aunt of a deceased cousin of Catriona Fraser's and cousin twice removed from Ken Fraser. Presumed dead."

"If anyone presumed me dead, that is hardly my fault," she declared. "And there is nothing illegal about my being here. It's not as though I came in disguise or outright lied. My only sin, as perceived by Clan Fraser of Red Dougal, was to marry outside the family and to marry a foreigner at that."

Everyone awake in the room watched her, saying nothing and waiting.

"Twenty-three years ago, I fell in love with a young artist by the name of Carlos Delacruz and, knowing my family would never accept him, we eloped to Venezuela. His family owned a coffee plantation near the Columbian border, and when he inherited the estate he proved an able businessman, and La Finca Delacruz flourished. Upon his death, I returned to Scotland, leaving the plantation in the capable hands of our manager. I knew there were only two living Frasers in our clan aside from myself, and that they had married and legitimately acquired Gleneagle Castle. I relinquished any interest I may have had many years ago when I left the Highlands. I wanted nothing at all to do with that accursed castle. But I wanted to meet the Frasers, my only surviving Scottish kin, without revealing my identity, it is true. What good would it have done to rehash the past? I was forgotten. I did not want them to think I was staking a claim to the castle and its gold. And I am not now."

"So why did you wish to meet them?" the chief inspector demanded.

"I was feeling nostalgic, I suppose, and perhaps a little unhinged by my husband's death. Carlos and I had a wonderful marriage, and I embraced my new family and adopted country with open arms. I changed my Gaelic name for Margaret to Margarita and took my husband's surname upon our marriage, as was natural. I never tried to hide, and no one in Scotland made a serious attempt to find me—obviously. Besides which, I was of legal age at the time."

Rex listened to the flow of flawless English. Just now and then was he able to detect a Scottish pronunciation or inflection, but twenty-three years of speaking Spanish seemed to have rid her diction of a distinct accent.

"I am a wealthy woman in my own right," she now shot at the chief inspector. "I have no need of a Scottish fortune. And therefore, no need to murder my kin."

"That's as may be," Dalgerry retorted. "The fact remains you were here under false pretences and never divulged your true identity to anyone—except perhaps the professor?"

"I did not betray you, Margarita," Cleverly said solemnly.

Rex switched his attention to the professor. It made sense that he would know who she was. Had he facilitated this arm's length meeting with her relatives?

"Professor Cleverly was sworn to secrecy," Margarita replied. "I wrote to him because I knew of his interest in Scottish genealogy, and asked him to look into my dying family tree and find out what he could. I have a daughter, Carlotta, and felt it was right she should know about her Scottish ancestry. I decided to revisit my first home. That's when I learnt the castle had been restored to the family. However, I did not hear about the gold until last night. I only knew that Humphrey had already been in touch with Ken and Catriona, having discovered some old documents that referred to one of our ancestors, and that he might be able to arrange an anonymous meeting here. Mr. Graves, our kind host, was organizing a Hogmanay party and had invited his new neighbours, the Frasers."

Rex felt slightly used. Cleverly had led him to believe Margarita was an old friend, and perhaps something more. He had been aware of an aura of mystery surrounding the lady and the exact nature of her relationship with the professor, but had assumed it to be out of a sense of delicacy, and not subterfuge. The professor did not meet his gaze.

"What you would have us believe, is that you had no reason to murder your kin."

"I came to see them alive and not dead, Chief Inspector." Margarita stood straight and regal in her black stilettoes and did not flinch.

"A whopper of a coincidence," he derided. "And you were not forthcoming with Detective Sergeant Milner. It was largely due to his diligence that we discovered your connection to your late relations." He scowled at her. "That will be all for now."

"Might we confer briefly?" Rex asked the chief inspector.

Dalgerry agreed. Margarita re-seated herself with dignity, head held high upon her slender neck. Dalgerry and Rex exited past Milner and entered the hall where they could speak in private.

"Did you discover anything else concerning that lady?" Rex asked.

"Not yet. Fortunately, I too have an aunt Maighread," the chief inspector told him. "I knew it was Gaelic for Margaret. You mentioned the name of Catriona Fraser's cousin's aunt in your extremely thorough statement. I thought Margarita Delacruz might be the right age for an aunt too. Since we had her date of birth, middle name, and where she was born, it was a simple matter for Milner to find her in the public records under Maighread Rose Fraser, born in Inverness. She said her husband died of a stroke. I wonder." Dalgerry bit his skewed lip, no doubt pondering the possibility of a poison dart in the man's bloodstream.

"I still don't think she could have murdered Ken Fraser, if Ace Weaver's memory is sound," Rex said.

"As sound perhaps as the other guests'. We have only a vague and conflicting timeline. After the lights went oot, most of the guests were at sixes and sevens. They weren't paying attention to anyone's movements."

Dalgerry flipped back the pages of his notepad. "You, Alistair, and John went to look for Ken Fraser, and Drew Harper stayed indoors to look downstairs. Why did he not go with the rest of you?"

"He would have, I expect, but he wanted to check downstairs first. He wasn't wearing appropriate shoes for trudging around in the ice. And then, of course, he found Ken in the broom cupboard."

"Of course," Dalgerry repeated meaningfully.

It was clear he did not like the house agent, perhaps because Drew drove a more expensive car and didn't keep such arduous hours as the chief inspector; or simply because Drew had shown a disrespectful attitude toward him. However, Rex had faith that Dalgerry possessed enough experience and maturity not to let petty emotions blind him to the facts of the case.

"You can tell your guests they can leave, but I'll want to talk to some of them again tomorrow, that is, later today."

Rex relayed the inspector's words to his guests, but asked first if any of them had thrown anything into the fire. They shook their heads as they rose from their seats and prepared to leave.

"Anyone who wishes to sleep over is most welcome," he added apologetically.

It appeared most of them just

wanted to get out of Gleneagle Lodge, and Rex could not blame them.

"My mum's expecting me," Flora said.

Rex recalled Dalgerry informing him that Flora had made a call to the Loch Lochy Hotel. Hamish and Shona would be aware of the new murders at the lodge.

He escorted the departing guests into the hall and helped Flora on with her coat. "That's a fine shawl," he complimented. "It's mohair, isn't it? Did you knit it yourself?"

"I did."

"Do you knit a lot?"

"I suppose."

"Just for yourself?"

"And for Donnie. I knitted a scarf for Jason but he lost it."

"Was it this lovely blue too?"

Flora gave him a befuddled look. "No. Purple and white."

"That was careless of him. My son

was always losing stuff. It's their age. It used to drive me bonkers."

Flora smiled wanly and thanked him again for his hospitality.

"Och, nonsense. Hogmanay was a sad event this year."

"It started out fun," Flora consoled him. "It's not your fault."

"I'm especially sorry because you knew the Frasers."

She looked startled. "What do you mean?" she faltered.

"Well, you met them before, at your parents' hotel. I was having dinner there."

"I didn't speak to them much then. Mum was so thrilled she was entertaining royalty," Flora said with irony. You know how she is. She was trying too hard to make them feel welcome. So I tried to keep out of their way this time."

No doubt Shona had thought having the castle's owners as regulars at the Loch Lochy Hotel would enhance its reputation.

"I liked them though," Flora hastened to add. "They weren't pretentious or anything."

Rex kissed her on the cheek and asked her to give his and Helen's regards to her parents, knowing they would be more than displeased with him for subjecting their daughter to danger once more.

"Jason," he addressed the approaching student, who had been talking to John and Alistair down the hall. "Did you mention your gold coin to the chief inspector?"

"Didn't have much choice, did I?" Jason groused. "Drew would have said something about it, I'm sure." He punctuated his statement by defiantly tooting with all his breath on a blowout, looking around to see where the house agent might be, but he was nowhere in sight. Rex thought he might still be in the library saying goodbye to Julie.

"I was asked to produce the coin." Jason looked crestfallen.

"Perhaps you'll get it back," Rex said.

"Fat chance."

Rex opened the front door and received a blast of cold air in his face. The porch light made the ice glisten on the path and he cautioned everyone to watch their step and drive carefully.

It transpired that Drew was dropping Margarita off at her hotel on his way home while Humphrey drove back to Edinburgh. Drew helped her on with her mink wrap and she breezed past Rex with the curtest of thank-you's. The house agent hurriedly shook his hand and followed her out the door, offering his arm to steady her in her high heels.

"Seems Drew likes rice, older women," Julie said, stomping her way up the stairs. "Her face looks tight, like she's had surgery."

"He's just being polite," Helen countered, clearly at the end of her patience with her friend. "Professor Cleverly has a long drive home and her hotel is on Drew's way."

"How convenient," Julie said snidely.

Rex sighed to himself. He had warned his fiancée not to interfere in Julie's love life, but it was in her nature to wish as much happiness on her friends as she had found for herself. Now look how it had ended! Like a damp firework that had spluttered and fizzled...

When all the guests who were departing had gone, he left Helen to finish making arrangements for the Weavers and went to find the chief inspector. Dalgerry was perusing his notepad in the kitchen and had taken off his coat, which lay draped over the back of a chair. Rex wondered how long he intended to stay and if he should offer more tea.

"May I conduct an experiment before you confiscate the rest of the items?"

"We are not appropriating anything further, Mr. Graves. We took Jason Short's penknife, the eye drops found in Ken Fraser's trench coat, his pipe, the contents of the ashtrays, and the Delacruz woman's cigarette holder, among other items. What is it you need?"

Rex indicated an unopened bag of fringed blowouts that had been brought in from the living room and left on the pine table. Every loose item of interest would have been bagged and removed for further examination. "I need one of those blow things that roll oot paper."

"Be my guest. Mind if I put the kettle on?"

"Go ahead. I was going to offer you tea." Rex tore apart the transparent bag of silver-striped blowouts in red, green, gold, and black, with corollas of matching metallic fringes. He pulled out a red blowout.

Dalgerry wandered over to his side after putting the kettle on the stove. "What are you going to do with that?" he asked.

Rex blew on the cardboard tube before answering. It made a raspy sound as the harlequin-patterned paper unfurled a tongue of about a foot long. "They are made with a tube, are they not? It's so obvious I missed it at first." He held it out to show the chief inspector. "They have a plastic mouthpiece you blow through and which fills the paper with air, *quod erat demonstrandum*."

"Aye. Silly wee things, if you ask me."

"Don't you see? One may have been used to fire a dart."

Dalgerry stared at him with bulging

brown eyes. The kettle started whistling. The chief inspector ignored it. "You may be on to something," he said at length. "But do you really think the killer used a party whistle to poison his victims?"

"One of the victims, anyway. It's the perfect cover. Who would suspect something so innocuous?"

"Who brought these noisemakers?"

"Jason, John, can't remember who else. Jason was blowing one just now in the hall."

"They were strewn all over the place." Dalgerry took the party blowout and rolled out the paper with his forefinger. "It's sealed at the bottom," he remarked. "I suppose the killer could have put a hole in it."

Rex took it back and pulled off the paper tongue and metallic fringes surrounding it, leaving the cardboard tube separate.

"Och, aye," Dalgerry said. He

walked back to the stove and silenced the screaming kettle.

"From a short distance, I imagine it would work. Let's find oot." Rex took the shiny coloured tube to the library and, opening his box of trout casts, disassembled one from its hook. The bob fly, a Black Zulu for use on dull windy days, had a varnished nose, a body of seal's fur, and a doubled red floss tail, and was designed to be tripped along the surface of a loch and mistaken by trout for a tasty insect struggling to take off from the water.

He was loath to destroy it, but needs must. He pulled out the plastic mouthpiece, inserted the artificial fly into the tube, replaced the mouthpiece, and blew with all his force. The simulated dart flew out the tube and landed undramatically a few feet away on the rug.

Dalgerry, who had joined him with a steaming mug of tea, scratched an ear. He spoke in a low voice so as not to wake Ace Weaver. In his excitement, Rex had forgotten all about the old man asleep on his daybed. "Well, technically it works, but would it really do the job?" the chief inspector asked.

"I'm sure more skill and finesse would be required. But, remember, we're not using a real dart that would have proper lift. The trajectory of the dart may only have needed to be a few feet. Ken Fraser wouldn't have seen it coming. And it would have avoided a struggle and the sound of one."

"An interesting hypothesis," the chief inspector allowed. "That one didn't make much of a sound. But why all the bother with darts and pipes in the first place? That's what stumps me."

Rex held up the festive tube. "By this means, the killer avoids contact with the victim and doesn't even need to be in the same room. Perhaps after the first killing the murderer got over his scruples and just jabbed Catriona's thumb. The plaster concealed the point of entry. Another perfect cover. No need to shoot the dart in that instance when a better alternative presented itself."

"Do we know for sure that Ken was killed first? The doctor couldn't tell as yet."

Rex shook his head slowly. "Not with absolute certainty."

Dalgerry clapped him on the shoulder. "Don't look so glum." He pointed to the decorative tube. "That could be the other half of our murder weapon." He set down his mug on Rex's desk and consulted his notes. "The first dart was allegedly found by Vanessa Weaver under Catriona Fraser's armchair, purposely hidden from view, or accidently kicked there and unrecoverable by the killer. The second dart was discovered in our imposter's handbag. I'm re-interviewing the lady later today."

"Where is she staying?"

"At a hotel near here. The Brambles."

"I know it." Rex recalled the ornate wrought-iron gate and profuse ivy clambering up the grey stone walls to the pigeon-walk balconies. A rather elegant establishment.

"Professor Cleverly is booked in there too. Separate rooms."

"Humphrey went back to Edinburgh."

"Abandoned the sinking ship, eh?"

"Was any tube that was missing its paper tongue taken away?" Rex asked. "And, if so, do you think you could you have the mouthpiece tested for DNA? Whoever blew it may have left some on it."

Dalgerry nodded assent.

Rex tried his experiment again, with similar results, except that this time when he blew, the tube emitted a sonorous tooting sound, like a horn, as had Jason's. He tried blowing a couple more times and found that if he channelled his breath in a more upward direction, it made the sound, otherwise it expelled air with only a rasping noise.

"Rex... What are you doing?" Helen asked from the doorway. "I heard noises from down the hall. You'll wake Ace."

"Och, he's dead to the world."

Helen gave her fiancé a quizzical look and then asked, "What's that in your hand?"

"One of those party blow things. Or part of it."

"Oh, I see," Helen said approaching on tiptoe so as not to disturb the invalid. "It's a makeshift blowpipe. Without the paper part, you're left with a cardboard pipe and a plastic mouthpiece. And it blends in with the spirit of New Year's Eve. Ingenious."

"Indeed."

"Does it work?"

"I had to use one of my trout flies as a substitute for a dart. They're not meant to sail through the air."

"Wouldn't Jason's empty Biro or Margarita's cigarette holder work as well?"

"They went to be tested for trace evidence of poison," Dalgerry informed her. "The lady'll have to inhale her cigarettes direct or else get another one."

"One of these would be more disposable," Rex said holding up his tube. "And everyone was blowing them. But if you can get DNA off one that just has the tube, it might point us in the right direction," he repeated to the chief inspector.

"Aye, that was a shrewd observation, Mr. Graves. We'll see what turns up."

"D'you have a suspect to match the DNA to?" Helen asked him.

"Not yet."

"Vanessa and Zoe are settled upstairs," she told Rex, going up to the daybed to check on Mr. Weaver, who, amazingly enough, had slept through the experiment.

"Well, I'll leave you both to your rest now," the chief inspector declared. "No sleep for me, I warrant!"

He thanked Helen for the tea and biscuits and set off after Detective Sergeant Milner, who informed his superior that he had been busy on the phone with HQ. Rex waved them off from the front door and then closed it with no small measure of relief.

The police and crime personnel had vacated the property leaving tape and fingerprint dust in their wake, as he saw when he toured the downstairs. The stone hearth had been swept clean, the ashes removed for sifting through for evidence.

"I'll ask Maggie Kerr from the

village to clean up this mess," he told Helen. "I think you should take Julie to my mother's in the morning and wait for me there."

"How long will you be?"

He could not say with any certainty. Dalgerry seemed to have gone from entertaining an intruder theory to championing an imposter one. Rex felt he was only humouring him about the party blowout in order to keep his own cards close to his chest. He also felt he was missing a vital clue. What was it that the chief inspector had said that might hold importance? Rex had not had time to write everything down. Yet, something had taken root in his brain and he was determined to weed it out.

"You look all in," Helen said. "You're so pale that the freckles are standing out on your face." She managed to persuade him to get a few hours' rest and he reluctantly agreed.

13
EVIL TIDINGS

At eleven o' clock the next morning, Rex and Helen sat at the breakfast nook. She had washed all the glasses by hand, and Rex insisted she leave the rest of the cleaning to Mrs. Kerr, who had been only too happy of the extra work, judging by her enthusiastic response when he had telephoned. No doubt her drunkard of a husband had blown through a big chunk of his labourer's wages for Hogmanay and the additional income was welcome.

It had been cold enough during the power cut for the food not to spoil in the refrigerator. The Weavers had left half an hour earlier, Ace having consumed a hearty breakfast and cheerfully reminisced about the earlier events of New Year's Eve, his memory apparently having erased the later ones. Vanessa saw fit not to remind him. "It'll only confuse him if I try to explain," she had confided to Helen and Rex.

Julie was still asleep, and Rex predicted she would spend ages in the bathroom as usual and use up all the hot water. He didn't expect the women's departure until after lunch at this rate. He prodded at his scrambled eggs. It was too soon for any news from Dalgerry. The chief inspector would be speaking to Margarita Delacruz during the course of the day and to Jason, who was supposed to turn in his gold coin. All Rex could do was wait on events unless he had any further flashes of inspiration at his end, or unless he remembered the niggling but faceless memory that continued to elude him.

Was it too early to ring Flora? Perhaps he should wait another half an hour. He fiddled with an intact party blowout, idly watching as his breath extended the paper tongue like an elephant rolling out its trunk, and mulled over why the murderer had picked his Hogmanay party to carry out his or her plan. He underlined one possibility in his notebook: Opportunity to approach the Frasers.

An intruder would have had to have known about the guest list. However, rumour was rife in Gleneagle Village. He couldn't post a letter without someone inquiring about the recipient and calculating how much time it would take to reach its destination, factoring in the vagaries of the weather, as though mail pigeons were the mode of transport in those parts. Outsiders, such as the villagers considered Rex to be, were a constant source of speculation and gossip. Perhaps Dalgerry was right about the significance of the van and the wool fragment.

"What are you going to do today?"

Helen asked, pouring more tea for them both. "Other than scribble away in your notebook, I mean."

"Hole myself up in the library and try to solve this case."

"What are you going to do for food?"

"There's loads left over. Don't worry, I won't starve. Perhaps you should take some of it back with you to Edinburgh."

"We could stay, you know." Helen sat back down at the table and sipped her tea out of one of the scalloped, rose-patterned cups.

"It won't be much fun for Julie here. Perhaps you two could go shopping on Princes Street. There are bound to be some sales."

Helen's face brightened. Then she frowned. "Will the shops be open on New Year's Day? I just don't want you to get lonely here by yourself."

"I'll have Mrs. Kerr for company if I

get desperate. I hope they haven't heard aboot the murders in the village. But I don't think she would have agreed to come if she knew."

"She'll see the tape and fingerprint dust."

"I'll tell her the Landseer was stolen."

"It's only a copy. Tell her some valuable law books went missing. That won't incite much interest in the village."

"Good idea, but it's only a matter of time until the truth gets oot."

Rex put his napkin on the table and rose from his chair. "I'll be in the library making some calls." He thanked her for breakfast and bent to kiss her full on the lips.

"I'm sure you'll solve this case," she said. "If Julie weren't here, I'd be glad to help."

Rex did a double-take. Helen actually looked a little regretful. "I'll keep you posted," he promised.

In the library, he dialled the Loch Lochy Hotel on his old-fashioned desk phone. Flora answered on the third ring in a business-like tone, stating the name of the establishment.

"Oh, hello, Rex," she said after he announced himself. "My mum's got me answering the phone in case it's reporters or nosy locals."

"Did you get any sleep, lass?"

"A little."

"What aboot Jason?"

"Oh, he left after dropping me off last night. I mean, early this morning. He had to drive to Inverness to get that French coin. He has to go down to the station today."

"Listen, Flora. I called to ask aboot that scarf. The one Jason lost. It may not be important. I just wanted to know when he lost it."

"Back in October, the day he found that coin, actually. Why do you ask?"

"And did you knit him another purple and white scarf just like it?"

"No, why? He shouldn't have been so careless." Flora sounded quite cross. "Did you find it?"

Rex hesitated. If the scarf had become entangled in the tree, why had Jason told Flora he had lost it? Losing a scarf did seem more careless than accidentally damaging it. Perhaps he had not wanted to admit he had been trespassing.

"Not exactly," Rex said in answer to the question of whether the scarf had been found. The chief inspector might not appreciate him discussing it, even if Flora had been the one to divulge the particulars. "I'm sure it isn't important," he reiterated.

"I won't mention any of this to Jason," Flora said. "He might get angry at me for bringing it up again. It took me forever to forgive him. Do you want to speak to my parents?"

Rex didn't and made a polite excuse about having to see Helen and Julie off. He promised to call back as soon as he heard anything to do with the case. No sooner had he hung up than his phone rang out the choral notes of "The Bonnie Banks o' Loch Lomond."

"Bad news, I'm afraid," Dalgerry told him. "Maighread Fraser, to use her given name, was found dead of an overdose in her hotel room this morning."

Rex hunched over the phone. "What did she overdose on?"

"We don't know yet. Maid service knocked on the door and went in when there was no answer. The girl found her in her nightdress dead under the covers. A small enamel pill box was on the bedside table."

"She had such a pill box in her handbag. The pills looked like aspirin."

"That's why we didn't take them

last night. She said she needed them. She swore aspirin and carbonated fruit juice at bedtime did the trick for a hangover. Personally, I prefer a greasy fried breakfast. One moment...," Dalgerry apologized.

Rex waited while he spoke away from the phone to a respectful male voice in the background.

"I never heard of anyone fatally overdosing on aspirin," Rex said doubtfully when the chief inspector came back on the line. "And I only noticed eight or so pills in the box."

"Perhaps she had an allergic reaction. Dr. Carmichael is looking into it."

The pathologist was having a busy start to the new year, Rex mused. Three deaths, and all guests at his party!

"According to Drew Harper, who dropped her off at the hotel, she was going to stay a few more days to make funeral arrangements for Ken and Catriona, being next of kin," Dalgerry informed him. "She said she would use a car service. Appears she was not contemplating suicide then."

"Did Drew take her up to her room?"

"No, left her at the front door to the hotel. It's still possible she committed suicide. She must have known she was a suspect: Her kin were murdered, she had come all the way from Venezuela to see them incognito, and a poison dart was found in her bag. She knew I wanted to question her today."

"Aye, it didn't look good for her," Rex concurred. "Even if she did lie only by omission and used her married name."

"Perhaps her nerve failed her. And she said she was 'unhinged' by her husband's death. Or his murder," Dalgerry said darkly. "DS Milner is trying without much success to get through to her hometown in Venezuela to track down Carlos Delacruz's death certificate and get more information. Of course, it's the first day of the year all over the world and people are not exactly busy at their desks."

"Or at the lab, I suppose." The second of January was also a bank holiday in Scotland, so a response might take a few days.

"No, nothing yet, except that the charred fragment of paper from your fireplace belonged to a roll-out whistle like the one you blew on. It still had the red metallic fringes attached."

"The other part of the tube used to shoot the dart." Good news indeed, Rex thought.

"It may be days, even weeks before I hear anything more," Dalgerry stated. "Depends on the backlog."

"Is the late Margarita Delacruz your prime suspect at this point?"

"Everything points to her. I can't trust an old man's memory, Mr. Graves, no matter how credible his story sounded and how adamant he was. And now her suicide, if suicide it is. Pity she didn't leave a note."

"That is strange, especially as she has a daughter. One whom she'd wanted to know about her Scottish heritage."

"DS Milner is attempting to contact her as we speak with his limited Spanish. He goes to the Costa del Sol every summer. Well, I best get on."

Rex entreated the chief inspector to call as soon as he heard anything further and ended the call reflectively.

Twas there that we perted in yon shady glen
On the steep, steep sides o' Ben Lomon'
Whaur in purple hue, the hielan hills we view

An' the moon comin' oot in the gloamin'.

Rex could not rid his mind of the words to the song. They kept returning insidiously. The ballad told of a woman grieving for her Jacobite lover taken to London for execution, and her sorrowful return to Scotland taking the low road used by commoners, while his head was displayed on a pike, one of many beheaded rebels, along the highway to Glasgow.

Sad that Maighread Fraser should return to the Highlands after so many years and meet a tragic end. Death from aspirin poisoning, either acute or chronic, was relatively rare, Rex confirmed upon researching the subject online. His brain worked feverishly. What if some other drug had been substituted? Something that looked like aspirin but was stronger? Then, just before bed, the unsuspecting victim had taken her hangover "cure" and was dead by morning.

He retrieved the jar of resolutions, which had been left on the living room shelf. He placed the fifteen pieces of paper face down on his library desk with the names on the back showing, and began to arrange them according to where he thought the guests had been standing when the knock at the door sounded shortly after midnight. None of the three Frasers' resolutions would ever reach fruition now, he realized with a cold feeling at the pit of his stomach.

The papers were about the size of business cards, cream in colour. He had divided two sheets of Gleneagle notepaper into sixteen pieces: one for each person and one left over. Most of the guests had only written their first names. Jason had added his last name, as had Zoe. Alistair had scrawled his unmistakable signature with customary flourish. Professor Cleverly had merely written his initials, H.L.C.

One piece of paper was blank on one side, where part of the watermark showed. Rex turned it over and saw spidery black letters. The message in Spanish contained the name Margarita and the word "amor." As far as Rex could fathom, it had something to do with the coming year bringing love and good health. Comparing the writing to the others, he found it to be in Cleverly's hand. The professor had written two resolutions, silly old beggar! That meant a resolution was missing from one of the other guests.

Glancing at the names, he quickly deduced it was Margarita's that was absent. Her resolution, he recalled, had been to take up painting. There had been no necessity that he could see for not leaving it with the others. Had she in fact written it down? Of that he was less sure. The fact remained there were fifteen pieces of paper, two of which were from Humphrey. And there was no blank message.

Rex contemplated the array of cards before him. Had she taken her own life out of fear of prosecution, guilt for her actions, or compounded grief over her husband's death? Was she in fact responsible for his death, as Dalgerry had suggested? Rex placed the blank-backed card to his far right on the desk in his re-enactment of where the fireplace would be and where Ace Weaver had insisted Margarita had been standing at the time of the knocking at the door. Cleverly's second piece of paper he positioned to the left, near where the living room door would be.

It occurred to him he should inform Cleverly of the news; if the police hadn't contacted him first. He called the number of the professor's Edinburgh flat and listened to the phone ring endlessly. Cleverly would have had a long drive home. He might still be asleep.

"Hello," a voice answered groggily at last.

"Humphrey, Rex here. Sorry to disturb you. Glad you got home all right."

"Easy enough drive in spite of the weather. Hardly any traffic except for police cars on the prowl for drunk drivers. Any news?"

"Aye, and it's sad news, I'm afraid. Another death. Chief Inspector Dalgerry informed me just now that Margarita succumbed this morning to an overdose." Rex heard a gasp and waited for the professor to collect himself.

"When I asked for news, I meant... I never imagined... Margarita! Dead? Are you sure? I cannot believe it. She was fine when I said goodbye to her last night at your door. Concerned aboot the investigation, of course, and upset over the death of her relations. She said she had a bad headache but would take her aspirin. I said I'd call today to see how she was. Oh, dear," Cleverly said in distress.

Rex recalled what he had deciphered in the message. In spite of his amorous intentions, Cleverly had let Drew drive Margarita to her hotel, no doubt under the circumstances choosing to distance himself from a key suspect.

"Humphrey, I have to ask, do you think Margarita was capable of suicide?"

Cleverly hummed and hawed. "Well, not to put too fine a point on it, insanity and suicide did run on that side of the Fraser clan. Margarita was a bit high-strung, I suppose. Do you really think she took her own life?"

"I'm exceedingly sorry, Humphrey. I understand you had feelings for the lady."

"I admit I was quite enchanted by her. A rather exotic creature, and such wit. What the French would call 'spirituelle.'"

Only an academic would strive for the *mot juste* at such a moment, Rex thought with mild cynicism. Judging by the resolution, the professor had entertained feelings stronger than friendship. "Humphrey, I need to ask you something—"

"One moment," interrupted Cleverly. "I need a wee dram of something to help with the shock."

Rex heard the *thunk* of the headset being deposited on a hard surface, and waited. When the professor returned, Rex explained he had reviewed the resolutions and found two by him and nothing from Margarita.

Cleverly took a gulp of whatever he was drinking, and said, "Now that you mention it, I did write one that I afterwards thought better of. I wrote another on a second piece of paper. The first was sentimental in nature," he said coyly. "And inappropriate for the occasion, I felt."

Rex reread the slip of paper in his hand. "You had romantic intentions towards Margarita?"

"That is so. Was so, I mean!" His old college friend sounded distraught.

"That explains the two notes written by you," Rex said gently. "But where's Margarita's? Did she throw it away? That's what I've been wondering." But perhaps this wasn't the right moment to quiz Cleverly.

"Ah, I might be able to help you there," the professor said before Rex could tell him not to worry about it; he would call again at a better time. "I'll be right back." Again Rex heard the sound of the phone placed on the desk or table, followed by a door creaking open. A minute later, Cleverly was back on the phone. "I inadvertently put Margarita's resolution in my spectacle case thinking it was my first try, which I was embarrassed to leave lying around."

"We found your spectacle case. Alistair probably thought nothing of the note. After all, we were looking for a murder weapon."

"It was tucked beneath the cleaning cloth," Cleverly explained.

"Thanks, Humphrey. I should not have bothered you with this just now. Let me know if you need anything or just want a sympathetic ear. Helen will call in the next day or so to see how you are." His fiancée was a professional counsellor, and it might do Humphrey good to talk to her. "She's driving back to Edinburgh today with Julie. They'll be at my mother's house in Morningside."

"You are too kind," the professor thanked him.

After they hung up, Rex returned

to his rectangles of paper, pushing them around in a pensive manner.

A tap sounded at the door and Helen walked in, dressed for departure. He relayed the news of Margarita's demise and asked if she would call Humphrey when she reached Edinburgh.

"Of course I will. Poor man. It was obvious he had feelings for her. But..." She sank into a chair. "A third death? I'm just glad it wasn't here. Suicide. Well, Margarita was a bit temperamental, I suppose."

"That's what Humphrey said. I think he used the word 'high-strung.'"

"Perhaps Chief Inspector Dalgerry should not have been so heavy-handed with her."

"He's not one for using kid gloves," Rex acknowledged. "But we don't know for sure it was suicide."

"Accidental?"

"Or murder."

"Oh, Rex. Surely not. I think it's best we go, after all."

"Don't you want lunch before you leave?" he asked, indicating her fleece jacket.

"I made sandwiches for the trip. I left yours in the fridge."

Rex got up and kissed her. "Most thoughtful, thank you. Now, don't worry. It'll all get sorted. Is Julie ready?"

"Yes, she's just collecting her things."

After helping the women take their luggage and the groceries to Helen's Renault, which she had parked out front in readiness, they said their goodbyes.

"Thanks, Rex," Julie said, adding with wry humour, "It's been a most murderous New Year!"

More than you might think, he thought. He would let Helen fill her in on Margarita's death on the drive back to Edinburgh. "You're welcome, lass," he replied in kind.

Helen shook her head, smiling in despair. "Call me when you get a moment. What should I tell your mother?"

"Just tell her the power went oot and nothing else. That will explain why you're taking the food back. I'll explain everything when I see her in person, hopefully tomorrow."

He waved them off calling warnings through Helen's open window to drive safely. Then, failing to get the chief inspector on the phone, he made a mug of tea and ate a sandwich standing up in the kitchen, pacing and thinking. His mobile phone rang and he hastened back to the table to retrieve it. He saw it was Dalgerry. Rex snatched up the phone, his pulse racing. That the chief inspector was calling again so soon signified an important development.

14
THE GLENEAGLE ARMS

"A new piece of information has just come to light regarding Maighread Fraser," the chief inspector informed Rex. "Her death just got a lot more complicated."

Rex digested the news and asked the obvious question, "Why?"

"Because methadone was found in her system," Dalgerry revealed. "From what I was told, and this may be crucial, methadone pills can be mistaken for aspirin. But they're much more potent, used for severe and lasting pain and to help get addicts off heroin. Only a few would have been needed to do the trick in our victim's case."

"So, the killer, if that's what we're looking at, would have needed a prescription?" Rex asked, hoping to narrow the list of suspects.

"Wish it was that easy, but you can get methadone on the Internet without a prescription. We've traced drugs back to online pharmacies as far away as North America and once to the island of Nevis."

"Never heard of it."

"It's a volcanic island next to St. Kitts in the Caribbean. Lord Nelson was stationed there as a young naval officer. Investigations are now more global, Mr. Graves. Truth be told, I liked it better in the old days of policing. Now I need a team of computer graduates to track down half the leads."

"I hear you. Are you ruling oot suicide?"

"If it was suicide, she had a better chance of success with methadone than aspirin. The paramedics reported there were four methadone pills found in the pill box by her bedside. You said you had noticed eight pills when you were searching the guests' personal possessions, right?"

"Correct. Margarita said they were aspirin. Presumably somebody switched them at some point."

"You have a verra suspicious mind, Mr. Graves," Dalgerry said with a chuckle. "However, you may be right. Why would she lie aboot the pills she was taking? Unless she intended to use them on someone, and the tables were turned, if you get my drift. Well, I best get on," he said in his customary leave-taking.

"One minute, Chief Inspector." Rex proceeded to fill him in on the meagre information he had gleaned, most notably the existence of a purple and white wool scarf that Flora Allerdice had knitted for her boyfriend, and which he had subsequently told her he lost in October.

"Did you tell her we may have found strands of wool from it on your deer trail?" Dalgerry asked warily.

Rex explained he had asked only in a roundabout way and not mentioned its connection to the evidence found that morning. Whether Flora had made the connection, he did not know.

"I'll be talking to the lad today. Thanks again."

Following the call, Rex asked himself who could have procured the methadone. Jason's dad kept a chemist shop, he recalled. And John Dunbar was a medic and therefore had access to pain-killers. As the chief inspector had pointed out, anyone could get hold of almost any type of drug these days, but ordering online would leave a paper trail, or at least a virtual one, and could take longer to procure. All this assuming Margarita was not knowingly carrying methadone in the first place...

At that point in his train of thought, he heard the roar of a luxury engine in the courtyard lower its volume to a powerful purr. Slipping on his tweed jacket, he went to see who his visitor might be. Upon opening his front door, he spotted Alistair's silver Porsche embellishing his driveway and watched as his friend emerged through the car door. Rex welcomed him inside and took his coat, glad of Alistair's genial company.

"I stayed over at John's parents last night," he said, following his host to the kitchen. "His mother fusses over me nonstop. So I thought I'd escape and come over to offer moral support."

"She probably loves the fact that you're a respectable advocate and drive a flash car."

"It probably sweetens the pill," Alistair agreed with a flash of malice in his smile. "His old man isn't so understanding of John and me. He's a downright crotchety so-and-so, truth be told. But he's an invalid. Fell off a scaffold three years ago and has constant back pain as a result."

"Talking of sweetening pills, or pills, anyway, it transpires that my guest from Latin America is now dead from an overdose."

Alistair's grey eyes clouded over as his mouth opened and stayed that way without speaking for a moment. "Margarita? You don't say." He plunked himself down on a kitchen chair and put a hand to his temple, where his leonine hair was receding. "Not the aspirin?"

"Methadone, according to Chief Inspector Dalgerry."

"That's what Frank takes for his back. What was Margarita using it for?"

"It's possible she took it thinking it was aspirin."

"Oh, I see." Alistair glanced at Rex. "You think someone put the methadone in her pill box knowing she was going to take aspirin before she went to bed?"

"We all heard her say that, didn't we?"

Alistair nodded, deep in thought. "Who actually took notice, I wonder?"

"Exactly."

"Where was she staying?"

"At a local hotel. Drew dropped her off on his way home. And Jason would have passed The Brambles when he drove to Inverness after leaving Flora at her parents'." Rex didn't bring up the coincidence of John Dunbar having a father who took methadone for pain management. Alistair, he knew from an earlier conversation, would never entertain the suspicion of his partner's possible involvement. In any case, Rex failed to find a motive on John's part for murdering the Frasers or their long-lost relative from Venezuela.

"Methadone is powerful stuff," Alistair remarked, brushing crumbs away on the pine table top. "Not something taken casually. John's dad is on permanent disability. He should really be in a home with full-time care, but the Dunbars can't afford it. His wife is run ragged looking after him. John does what he can, of course."

Rex blinked at his friend and legal colleague. Alistair had just unwittingly supplied a motive for John. Money to pay for his father's care.

"Put some coffee on, old chap," Alistair said more brightly. "Else I'll have to prop open my eyes with matchsticks." He went on to lament about how much Scotch he'd had to drink the night before and how he had been unable to get adequate sleep on the Dunbars' lumpy sofa, especially since Snowdrop, their fluffy white cat, had insisted on trying to nap on his face. Rex ceased listening as he wrote "matches, lighter!!!" in his notebook, excitedly dotting each exclamation mark.

"Making progress?" Alistair asked with interest, breaking off his tale of nocturnal woes.

"Maybe. Thank you for reminding me of something Dalgerry said last night regarding ashtrays. It had slipped my mind until now, but it's been nagging at me because I felt deep in my bones it might hold some significance."

"Glad to be of assistance, old fruit," his friend said in a puzzled tone. "So. Any chance of that coffee?"

"Oh, right." Rex busied himself with preparations at the coffee maker, forgetting just how many spoonfuls of ground Columbian he put in the filter. "Helen made sandwiches before she left. Would you like one?"

"I thought we'd go to the Gleneagle Arms for lunch. They serve the best Cullen skink in the Highlands." A gastronome, Alistair always knew where to find the best food, just as he knew all the best places to shop and go on holiday.

A Guinness certainly appealed to

Rex, and he had only eaten the one sandwich. He too loved the smoked haddock, potato and onion soup at the Gleneagle Arms. "Sold," he said, "If it's open today." He had never known it to be closed. "In any case, I need you to act as a sounding board for my theory on the murders. But I have to wait for Mrs. Kerr from the village who's coming to clean. She shouldn't be long now. Don't tell her aboot the murders, by the way. She might not stay otherwise."

"What about that police tape?" Alistair asked, nodding at the kitchen door leading outside. "Bit of a giveaway, isn't it?"

"Helen made the same observation. I could take it down, but I daren't just yet, in case the investigators need to come back."

"Did Helen and Julie get off okay?"

"Julie was a bit subdued. Not surprisingly, what with the murders and her falling oot with Drew." Rex poured

Alistair's coffee into a blue ceramic bowl with a handle.

"That was a short-lived Highland fling!" Alistair said with Byron-esque wit. The Highland Fling was a dance.

"Aye, sadly for Julie. Here, this should set you up." Rex placed the large mug in front of his friend and went to fetch the milk from the refrigerator. "That must be Mrs. Kerr now," he said, hearing a stuttering car engine out front. "Good." He was ready for a pint. "I'll go and give her instructions."

He met the sturdy Mrs. Kerr in the hall. She dumped her large carrier bag of cleaning supplies on the stone floor and unknotted the headscarf under her all but non-existent chin, proffering the customary Hogmanay greetings and commenting on the dreary weather. Her wiry grey hair sprouted around her face where the small features congregated at the centre, the surrounding skin a mottled expanse of bumps and depressions, putting Rex in mind of a scrubbed potato.

Rex enumerated what was required of her, explaining that the police had been to investigate the disappearance of some law books, weighty tomes of reference written by scholars on the subject of feudal justice.

"I dinna ken what they would want wi' those," she remarked. "Weel, less to dust! Long as they dinna come back to rob me of ma virtue!"

"Slim chance of that," Alistair, the master of undertone, murmured as he came up behind Rex and grabbed his coat off the polished mahogany stand.

Rex admonished him with a mock-stern look. "Set the alarm if it'll make you feel more secure," he advised her. "I'll be gone an hour or so. We'll be at the Gleneagle Arms. You have my number."

"If you see ma Willie, shoo him oot

o' there, will ye? The pub's open today, reit enough, and he'll be the first one in it."

"Open? Grand," Alistair said rubbing his hands in anticipation. "Happy Hogmanay to you, Mrs. Kerr."

"And tae ye."

He and Rex exited the front door and sauntered forth into the bleak day that threatened rain. The ice was melting, and they stepped carefully to Alistair's Porsche, avoiding the puddles.

"Off to the local pub in style!" Rex said as he skirted around to the passenger side. Alistair beeped open the doors and Rex eased himself into the new-smelling leather upholstery. Alistair had owned the car for a couple of years, but it retained the distinctive luxurious scent.

"You could afford a car like this, Rex," his friend said, pulling his long limbs into the driver's compartment and strapping himself in. "You're far too big for that Mini Cooper. It pains me every time I see you get in it."

"It is too cramped for me," Rex agreed, "But it's easy to park and extremely fuel efficient." However, more often than not he took the train to Derby to visit Helen, a more comfortable alternative. "And I cannot afford a Porsche, not with maintaining this money pit, the upkeep of my mother's house, and the wedding."

Alistair was to be his best man. Rex and Helen had also invited John, Flora and Jason, and Humphrey "& guest." Well, Margarita would not be attending now. He trusted the others would be present at the big day, barring further complications.

Alistair swung the sports car around in the courtyard and began the climb up the gravel driveway to the slushy road winding its way to Gleneagle Village. Grimy ice laced the tarmac and glinted in the muddy verges where bluebells blossomed in early summer. On a day like today it was hard to picture the transformation the warmer months brought to the countryside, especially when the pall of murder hung over the view.

Rex's companion, sensitive to his moods and methods, refrained from interrupting his reverie with idle chatter, and soon they were entering the village, where the few people abroad carried umbrellas.

Alistair parked on the road outside the Gleneagle Arms, wedged between Murray's Newsagent's and a modest house with dingy net curtains. There was little through-traffic, particularly on New Year's Day. Rex got out of the car and felt the raw newness that the first of January always held for him. He stooped under the grey stone lintel and entered the pub, followed by his friend, who also had to watch his head as he crossed the threshold.

The cramped quarters compressed the ale fumes and smoke from the stone hearth, and Rex knew from experience that the combined odour would cling to his clothes all day, not altogether pleasantly. When he was here he always felt as though he were in a horror film where the lost traveller stumbles into a pub in the remotest part of the Highlands and feels several pairs of eyes drilling into his back while the locals make menacing comments in unintelligible Gaelic. And this time was no exception as he and Alistair settled into a corner, although there were fewer customers than usual. He thought the Gleneagle Arms should be featured in Zoe's television series. The low-beamed ceiling and small windows accentuated the gloom within the dank walls, giving the place just the right atmosphere for a murder mystery.

"Guid day tae ye," the scowling publican greeted them in perfunctory tones.

"And to you, my good man," Alistair urbanely replied. "My friend here will have a Guinness and I'll take a Glenfiddich. And we wish to order the soup advertised on your board."

The Cullen skink was consumed under suspicious stares, but Alistair's eulogies concerning the soup managed to thaw the landlady's frozen demeanour by a couple of degrees. During lunch, he listened to Rex lay out his conclusions regarding the recent triple deaths, and declared them to be sound, if more than a little startling.

Rex roundly agreed. "The difficulty will be in presenting them in such a way as to persuade the Chief Inspector Dalgerry to change the focus of his investigation."

Not an easy task, he anticipated.

15
CONCLUSIONS

When Rex returned from the Gleneagle Arms, having thanked Alistair for lunch and seen him off, he went straight to his library, which he had asked Mrs. Kerr to clean first. He could hear the hum of the vacuum cleaner upstairs. The wood exuded an aroma of beeswax furniture polish and a hint of lavender, and he spent a few moments putting objects back in their proper place and straightening pictures, lest they provide a distraction. The important task he was about to undertake would require all his concentration.

He had stuck to one pint of Guinness at the pub to keep a clear head, though he had been sorely tempted to have two. He longed for a smoke of his pipe but resisted.

Sitting behind his desk and stretching his fingers, he prepared to commit to paper his conclusions for the benefit of Chief Inspector Dalgerry. He drew his Gleneagle Lodge notepaper toward him, able to write in longhand with more fluidity than when he typed on a keyboard, and began with the date, that of January first. The letter continued thus:

Dear Chief Inspector,

Upon considerable thought, and based on the information available to me, I feel I am now able to offer a possible hypothesis with regard to the perpetration of the murders here at Gleneagle Lodge and at The Brambles hotel. I have to say it pains me in no small measure to finger the individual, but as an instrument of the law I am duty bound to voice my suspicions. Let me start with the first clue that set me on the path to my final deduction, and which was also, curiously enough, the last clue to occur to me as such. I make reference to the matches in the ashtray by the living room fireplace.

Since the beginning of the night, Margarita Delacruz was smoking a cigarette in her elegant black lacquer holder. She was using the box of matches on the mantelpiece. However, at the juncture where Alistair and I were conducting a search of the guests' handbags and pockets, she was offered a light from a lighter monogramed in gold with her initials.

It occurred to me that if someone had fetched her lighter for her from her evening bag, that person would have had an opportunity to plant or hide the dart used on Ken Fraser, and even substitute methadone for the aspirin. As for what could have happened to the aspirin, it could have been swallowed without serious detriment to the killer. When it was Margarita's turn to be searched, we found her pill box. We took her word for it that the pills inside were aspirin, but by that point they might, unbeknownst to her, have been methadone.

Why switch mode of death from a poison to a drug?

My theory is that the killer came with a contingency plan. AND THAT PERSON HAD TO HAVE KNOWN ABOUT MARGARITA'S 'WEE CURE'. Methadone requires a while to take effect, whereas curare immediately incapacitates the victim, rendering them unable to react or request assistance and, finally, to breathe, even as the heart continues to beat.

I further submit that the killer saw an earlier opportunity and acted upon it. I refer to the mix-up with the New Year resolution cards. Margarita's is missing. She might have decided not to put hers with the others, but I failed to find any logical reason why. Her resolution was not personal in nature, nor did it commit her to a resolution she could have felt unequal to fulfil. And yet, another guest wrote two, claiming the first was inappropriate. In that event, it would be only natural to take back the discarded card so no one could see it. This did not happen. The person "mistakenly" picked up Margarita's.

Again, why?

What if Margarita had put her signature on the back of her card, as had Alistair Frazer? A lady as formal in manner as Señora Delacruz might well have done so. Her signature might have value for someone. She was the third surviving member of the Red Dougal clan of Fraser. Old French gold had been proven to exist at Gleneagle Castle, thanks to Jason Short's metal detector. A poem translated from the Gaelic by Professor Cleverly pointed to its burial there, as did a diary entry written by a priest in 1786.

The professor was also able to

inform us that the poison used on Ken and Catriona Fraser was curare, and even how this fatal poison was typically administered. He was, in fact, so helpful that one might never suspect him of being the killer. And yet, 'The longer the pipe, the greater the velocity,' he said, or words to that effect, never suggesting a short tube might do the trick, and thereby seeking to mislead.

Since he was standing nearest the hall, he had offered to answer the door when a knock was heard shortly after midnight. He might have seen Ken leave the living room and, with the power out, seized his opportunity. The knock at the door could have been Ken bumping into the door in his inebriated state. Here is how I envision the scene:

After Cleverly was in the hall and out of sight, he set down his candle and, aiming the party tube, struck at Ken with the dart from several paces away, an easy enough shot. No struggle was involved, and therefore no noise except for the sound of Ken slumping to the floor. Cleverly opened the door at that point, as suggested by the draught, and dragged Ken into the broom cupboard. These sounds were covered by the storm and by conversation going on inside the living room. During this time, he said he was searching outside. He may have observed the overgrown vine, which he said was hitting the door, when he first arrived at the party. By the time Jason went to the cloakroom, Ken Fraser was nowhere to be seen.

Then, while most of the men were searching for Ken, and Helen and the other guests were either in the kitchen or seated around the coffee table, the professor approached Catriona in her armchair and inserted poison in her thumb. A prick in the existing cut would have sufficed and, in her deep sleep, she did not react loudly enough for anyone to hear.

Luck was with Cleverly even though he had no doubt anticipated more people at the party. The lack of light compensated for the diminished number of guests as potential suspects, although he would have counted upon dimmed lighting and the blowing of party horns to carry out his plan. Had the dart used on Catriona not been found, he may well not have revealed his knowledge of curare. He no doubt intended to dispose of both darts. His luck, fortunately for us, did not extend this far, since he must have dropped the one dart and been unable to retrieve it in the dark.

Later, as he said goodbye to Margarita, he advised her to take adequate "aspirin" for her hangover headache and get a good night's rest, secure in the knowledge that, with her dead, she could not incriminate him if she remembered his having fetched her lighter from her bag, where he had hidden Ken's dart. It might even be supposed she committed suicide out of remorse for murdering her relatives. If ever he had feelings for Margarita, they were overridden by fear and greed. Perhaps she had spurned him, adding fuel to the fire?

The professor asserted that his first resolution was sentimental and he had second thoughts about presenting it. I came to doubt his story. Humphrey is not a man prone to spontaneous declarations of love, to the point of making such a declaration public. This was a ruse for the purpose of substituting it for Margarita's signed piece of paper, and not so he could secure a keepsake.

Perhaps a search of his flat or university rooms will provide further answers and reveal a motive for all three murders, for I am convinced

Margarita Delacruz did not die from suicide. At one point, I wondered if she was in on the plot with Cleverly, who subsequently eliminated her out of fear of discovery, but I concluded her involvement was unlikely. She had not appeared interested in exploiting any gold hidden at the castle, believing it cursed, and superstitious of its power to destroy the Red Dougal clan.

I strongly suspect the murders have something to do with this Jacobite gold and Professor Cleverly's keen interest in it, regardless of any direct monetary value it might have for him. He appeared last night to be heavily invested in its history, indeed passionate. I would look to ambition as motive.

In the fervent hope that these observations serve to be of some small assistance to you in your investigation, …

Rex signed off with the usual formalities after reading over his letter, and folded the sheets of notepaper into the matching envelope with the intention of delivering the missive in person.

There remained some unresolved aspects to the case. For instance, had Margarita forgotten about the lighter? The act of forgetting such minutiae had happened to Rex numerous times. Only the other day he could have sworn he had taken a chicken out of the freezer to thaw, only to find approaching the dinner hour that he had not in fact done so. Helen had been furious. Well, as furious as she ever got. And then she had laughed and called him a senile old git. He smiled and glanced at his watch. She and Julie would be in Edinburgh by now, all being well.

Or had Margarita thought the lighter incident irrelevant to the investigation, not once suspecting

Cleverly? In any case, her friend had betrayed and used her for his own ends. Ends that had yet to be fully exposed and proven.

The matter was now out of his hands. He would close up the house and return to Edinburgh after putting the letter in Dalgerry's possession, and then salvage what remaining time he had left with Helen. Cleverly would get his comeuppance—or not.

16
AULD LANG SYNE

OLD AND NEW MYSTERY SOLVED? Professor Humphrey Cleverly, a lecturer of history at the University of Edinburgh is charged with murdering the heirs to Gleneagle Castle in Inverness-shire. His motive: To garner glory for recovering part of the lost Jacobite gold rumoured still to be buried at Loch Arkaig in Lochaber, Scotland...

Rex set aside the *Sun* tabloid, which Helen had picked up at the Derby train station when she saw the story, and pondered the events of the past fortnight. Cleverly's DNA on the plastic mouthpiece of a tube missing its paper blowout and containing a microscopic feather fibre had substantiated Rex's hypothesis and had served as grounds for the search of the professor's flat. This in turn had revealed a typed document taped behind the back of a drawer, and which read:

In the event of my demise, I, Maighread Rose Delacruz, née Fraser, being of sound mind, do bequeath my Scottish estate, if such should come into my possession, in its entirety, to my dear friend Humphrey L. Cleverly in gratitude for his help and kindness. (Signed) *Margarita R. Delacruz*

The significance of Margarita's missing, and now recovered, resolution was at present abundantly clear. Cleverly had pretended to have taken it in error, but in actuality he had stolen it because Margarita had written her signature on the back, and in those moments at the party the professor had seen a way to acquire the castle and, more importantly, the historic treasure.

He mentally applauded Cleverly's cunning.

A document expert had compared the signature on the will, which was pre-dated a week before her death, to the one in her passport and in the hotel register, and to samples sent from Venezuela, and had found it to be a passable forgery. In addition, a container of methadone among discarded letters and other refuse belonging to the professor had been found in a wheelie bin in the vicinity of his flat.

Cleverly had confessed when confronted with the evidence against him. He had asked Chief Inspector Dalgerry during a final interview if Rex had solved the case. The chief inspector had conceded that Mr. Graves had indeed done so, "for the most part." The professor seemed to derive pleasure from that, and reportedly said, "Tell Rex I take my hat off to him. He often got the better of me in debates. He has a very sharp mind behind that placid exterior." Dalgerry had said he was forced to agree.

"What are you chuckling at?" Helen asked as she cleared the breakfast table.

"My phone conversation with the chief inspector."

"Thanks to you, once again, he caught the murderer." She glanced through the window. "Well, the weather's finally cleared up. Do you still fancy a walk up to the castle?"

"I do. I want to see the old place again now that the case is closed. And I'm truly glad you were able to visit this weekend so you can go with me."

Dressed in hiking boots and warm waterproof clothing, they trudged up the wooded slope, sliding and slipping in the mud. The deer trail they followed was a continuation of the one Jason had admitted to taking when his scarf snagged on the tree branch back in the autumn. Another false lead in the first two Fraser murders had been the tyre marks on the road, which had been traced to a utility vehicle sent to mend the power line, and whose driver had stepped out briefly.

A cold wind seared Rex's lungs as he ascended the hill, although the sun shone wanly through the dense clouds. The rain and sleet had held off but left evidence of their recent force in the sodden undergrowth and brimming streams rushing down to the loch. By the time the couple reached the top, they were panting and leg sore. Helen leaned against the gnarled trunk of an oak tree to catch her breath, her cheeks a bright pink. After a short break, they set off again to cover the final stretch to the castle.

Assailed by sudden wind gusts, the sixteenth century ruin stood gray and forlorn on its vantage point overlooking bracken-brown glens and hills patched with the last of the snow. White-capped mountain peaks sparkled in the distance. Rex attempted to picture Gleneagle Castle standing proud and intact all those centuries ago, the high stone walls, stepped at the roofline, culminating in two tall chimneys billowing smoke either side of the tower.

Margarita Delacruz would no doubt have inherited the castle by virtue of being the sole surviving heir of the disfavoured branch of Clan Fraser. Perhaps now it would be put up for auction or claimed for conservation by the National Trust for Scotland, or even condemned in the interest of public safety. The stairway spiralling to the top of the tower had crumbled and made climbing hazardous. Whatever the outcome, Rex hoped he would be able to enjoy the tranquility of his country retreat a while longer, or at least until reporters and treasure hunters descended upon the valley.

The ruin was a disappointment up close, both in size and grandeur, lacking the perspective of the setting. He bowed his head beneath the low arched doorway leading into the cobblestone courtyard crowned with dilapidated battlements. Inside the narrow keep, the enclosed air felt chill and damp, but at least he and Helen were sheltered from the frigid breeze.

"We could be standing on a fortune," she said, stamping her booted foot on the large worn flagstones. "I still can't understand why Humphrey resorted to murder," she mused aloud, staring at the ground, as though mesmerized by bags of gold coin and bullion. "He would still have managed to get his name in the history books."

"He wanted to get full credit for finding the gold. According to a letter discovered among Humphrey's rubbish,

Ken and Catriona planned to write a book aboot Gleneagle Castle's colourful history and the gold supposedly buried here. They'd already found a publisher. Ken was seeking to solicit Humphrey's permission to use his translations of the Gaelic poem and relevant passages from the priest's diary that were written in Latin. But there was no mention of a share in the proceeds from the book or joint authorship with Humphrey."

"And yet it was Humphrey who authenticated the documents and solved the riddle," Helen pointed out. "Why didn't he write a book himself?"

"Ken and Catriona would have beaten him to the punch. They'd already done the research on their ancestors. The Frasers' account would have had wider appeal. It was their own blood line that was the subject, and they had a direct and personal connection to the famous treasure."

Helen sighed, her breath visible in

the cold air. "Obviously the letter was not well received."

"Spite got the better of my old friend. As for Margarita, I expect he could have persuaded her to lay claim to the castle and then let him take care of the excavation and publicity while she returned to her adopted home. But he must have thought it was too great a risk to let her live, in case she ever guessed his role in the first two murders and denounced him."

"But committing the murders right on your doorstep!"

"Where else would he have had the opportunity to murder the Frasers among a large group of people, diluting suspicion on himself? But for the storm, there would have been more guests at the party. Framing Margarita only adds to the cowardly and despicable nature of his actions. And then to kill her too... It all goes to show how desperate he must have been, or deranged."

Professor Cleverly would likely serve the rest of his days in prison or in a psychiatric ward.

Rex cast his mind back to his student days and shrugged dispiritedly. "I lost contact with Humphrey over the years. I imagine he became bitter, being passed over within the history department and never achieving the recognition he craved. Sad, really. He had no family or real interests ootside his scholarly pursuits. His academic standing was everything and once again he saw his hopes dashed."

Driven by ambition, Cleverly had wanted to leave his indelible footnote in history. Now he would be remembered more for his heinous crimes than for his valuable contribution. The West Highland Museum in Fort William had acquired the priest's written collection, including the diary and poem.

"Oh, don't feel too sorry for him. You were at university together and had an equal chance at success. You took silk and are now a Queen's Counsel. He could have made head of department or dean. Well, look at him now. Even obscurity would have been better than notoriety."

"Aye. Some things are better left alone."

With a final glance at the weathered flagstones concealing who knew what, they turned their backs on the ill-fated castle and headed home to the lodge.

THE END

THE AUTHOR

C. S. Challinor was raised and educated in Scotland (St. George's School for Girls, Edinburgh) and England (Lewes Priory, Sussex; University of Kent, Canterbury: Joint Hons Latin & French). She also holds a diploma in Russian from the Pushkin Institute in Moscow. She now lives in Southwest Florida. Challinor is a member of the Authors Guild, New York.

61140455R00203

Made in the USA
Middletown, DE
17 August 2019